COFFEE, TEA OR MURDER ME

PERSEPHONE PRINGLE COZY MYSTERIES: THREE

PATTI LARSEN

Copyright © 2021 Patti Larsen

All rights reserved.

Thanks, Kirstin!

ISBN: 978-1-989925-78-2

CHAPTER ONE

Mom and Ralph's cheery duo on speakerphone always made me grin, the sound of someone cutting their lawn in the background reminding me spring was here now that we'd passed into April and another gorgeous Maine summer around the corner, though my mother and her new (well, compared to Dad who she'd been with thirty-seven years before he passed) husband would soon be heading home from their winter in Florida.

"How are the girls, honey?" My mother's question caught me a little flat-footed, though it was hardly a surprise she'd ask since it was a standard query from her every time we talked. While not quite your typical make-you-cookies grandmother, more inclined to learn to sail or

1

bungee jump or take a safari in Africa while roughing it in a tent and carrying her own food and water, Marigold Pringle (now Stoddard) never failed to ask after my daughter and the young woman whose estate they both lived on.

"Callie and Thalia are fine, Mom," I said, stroking Belladonna's soft, white fur when the cat rolled over to allow me the privilege of accessing her belly. She blinked those huge, green eyes at me, giant yawn showing her many pointed teeth and bright pink tongue that matched her triangle nose. Our sessions were over for the day, my adopted friend turned therapy cat (her idea) never failing to bring peace and focus to my clients who adored her more than me, I was sure. I took advantage of that offer from her myself as, not for the first time and certainly not the last, I pondered why my girls—yes, Thalia Vesterville was as much my daughter as my biological kid and had been since they met at age six—had, as yet, to come clean with me and tell me about the real nature of their relationship. Something I'd kept to myself because no way was I outing either of them until they were ready to tell me otherwise. It just made talking with Mom a little uncomfortable. I was excellent at keeping secrets, part of my job. But when my heart was involved, I fought an odd and nagging anxiety

I'd accidentally blurt something I wasn't supposed to at the most inopportune time.

Therapist, heal thyself of thy fears already.

"I'm sure they're having just a grand adventure," Mom gushed.

"That big old place," Ralph said, his deeper and lovely tenor joining her more enthusiastic alto. "I've always wondered what secrets might be hiding in Vesterville House."

Mom giggled, the sound of her smacking him on the shoulder (her favorite expression of adoration he accepted with a smile on his white-bearded face) loud and clear over the phone. "Maybe they'll let us poke around when we get home."

How was it I ended up the most mature of our particular family? No clue.

"I'm sure you can ask them when you're back next month," I said.

"Such a burden to bear for that poor girl," Mom said then. "I don't envy her even a little, Persephone. Thank goodness she has our Callie to help her."

Tell me about it, though Thalia Vesterville, orphan and now heiress to the entire Vesterville fortune of old New England money, had shown a surge in her self-growth the last few months since she'd been named the sole inheritor with her grandfather's passing. I tried not to think about the events that led her to that position or the handsome uncle of hers who was not only far too young for me (sigh, Gaines, yum) but so far out of reach and propriety and every other reason I shouldn't have been thinking about him including the circumstances of his exit from Wallace. Instead, a soft hum from my phone created the perfect distraction when my alarm went off.

Just as Mom spoke again. "We're going to be late for Bingo night," she said. "Ralph promised me he'd let me have his lucky dabber, so we'd better go. Love you, honey!"

I didn't even get to say goodbye, Mom hanging up, Ralph's voice echoing in the background as the line went dead. The snort that escaped made Belladonna twitch, eyes opening in suspicion, purr softening to a dull murmur. "Bye, Mom," I said. Rubbed the kitty's tummy one more time before kissing her forehead. "I'm going out for a bit," I said. "You have a great sleep."

She seemed to realize I was leaving, rolled over, and hopped from the kitchen peninsula where I'd answered Mom's call before strolling to the sofa in the nearby living room and making herself at home on the big, fluffy white pillow Calliope had bought just for her, silver princess crown embroidered on the surface with "Your Highness" printed beneath.

I could swear the cat knew what it said because she claimed it instantly and no one else was allowed near it. Not spoiled or anything, right?

I was already at the door, keys in hand, my black leather motorcycle jacket (no, I didn't ride, I just loved the look) over jeans and a T-shirt my choice for my evening out, when someone rang the bell. Knowing I had little time—the engagement my alarm reminded me of had me tsking at the interruption—I opened the door without checking to see who might be behind it. Which meant, when my gaze settled on my ex-husband, I was positive my reflexive smile faltered enough it hurt him.

I didn't mean it. Trent Garret and I might have parted ways—my idea, yes—after twenty-four years together, but I wished him well. The thing was, I knew how much he disapproved of so many things about my life, both pre- and post-divorce, that having interactions with him had that awkward uncomfortableness that sometimes felt like he was a school principal trying to figure out what to do with a carefree and independent teenager more than an ex-husband having an adult conversation with his former wife.

While I was the adult in my particular unit,

Supervisory Special Agent in Charge Trent Garret of the FBI (and whatever other fancy-shmancy titles or accolades or assorted awards he carried around with him like he bore it all in physical weight on his shoulders and face) was the most adulty adult I'd ever met. To the point that I internally flinched from the dour and melancholy expression on his face, the lines on his forehead creased in that perpetual worried look that seemed to carry him through life.

Now, to be fair, the man chose to keep our family in Wallace through his entire career, opting to travel when needed instead of uprooting us, and still managed to climb the ladder at the Bureau to the point he led a team that hunted some truly horrific people around New England. So, the fact he appeared to bear the full load of humanity's wretchedness across his average shoulders, the proof of it laced liberally as silver through his dark hair, wasn't just earned, it was a badge of honor as impressive as the one he wore on his belt under his gun.

"Hey, Seph," he said in that middling alto of his, one hand rising and falling. At least he'd taken off his wedding ring finally. That made me happy enough despite the unexpected visit I smiled back and stepped into the entry to allow him to follow. He did, nodding thanks, his handful of inches in height over me almost eliminated by the height of my boots. "Sorry to just barge in like this. I was hoping we could talk."

"I'm on my way out," I said, sudden tension knotting my stomach. Trent never just stopped by to talk. In fact, I hadn't seen him in months, despite living in the same town, blissfully single and never encountering him regardless of where I went or what I did. More proof, as far as I was concerned, we'd never really been the kind of couple who would have been friends let alone gotten married if we'd thought the whole thing through.

She appeared like magic, her white fluffiness winding with delighted aggression between his suited legs, Trent's eyes narrowing and a giant sneeze escaping. I had to fight off the giggle at his instant allergic reaction to Belladonna while she continued to show him affection he could never return without a giant dose of meds.

"You got a cat." He choked, coughed, backed out onto the step again, sneezed violently.

Whoops and shrug. I shooed her into the house, closing the door behind me. "Yeah." Didn't apologize, despite his disapproving look. This was *my* house. *Mine*.

Feeling protective of your freedom for some reason, Persephone Pringle? Might want to work on that. Because how I felt wasn't going to change his judgment even a little.

Trent slowly recovered, brushing at the hair clinging to his legs. "It's about Callie." What about my kid? Okay, our kid. "But I guess it can wait." He sounded sad enough I relented, though I refused to continue feeling sorry for him when he was a grown man, after all, and it wasn't like I'd minced words or left him wondering what I wanted all along. Like the six or seven million times I asked him if he was happy, told him I wasn't. Only stayed because he said he'd do whatever I wanted to keep us together. Resulting—the therapist in me wailing her warnings for years—in only deeper determination and, ultimately, the end of us.

I knew many people thought I was selfish and maybe trying too hard with my blonde pixie cut and gleefully acquired tattoo collection and skinny jeans. Surely being this happy on my own meant there was something wrong with me? Not my problem.

"Why don't I come by the office tomorrow?" I headed for my SUV, ending the conversation, furious with myself suddenly, with him, too, for being put into the position where I felt like I was the bad person for wanting to live my truth. Clearly, I had a lot of healing left to do if the spiral of thoughts around my ex led me so quickly into a knee-jerk reaction when he hadn't done a thing really, to trigger it. If anything, Trent was one of the nicest people I'd ever met.

Which meant, of course, I was the opposite, right?

Growl.

He didn't respond with words, just stood there a moment, that mournful look I wanted to smack from his face placing everything that had ever been wrong with us into my possession like a pile of hot bricks I would never be able to set down before he finally nodded and got back in his sedan, driving away while I stood in my driveway, forcing deep breaths and contemplating my strategy to shed my ex-husband from my psyche forever.

My phone vibrated in my pocket.

Great. Not only was I unexpectedly dealing with all the emotional turmoil that still surrounded my love life, I was going to be late.

CHAPTER TWO

It wasn't until I was driving toward Vesterville House I had a horrible, crushing thought, shattering the anger I lingered in while I crossed town to pick up the girls. Trent's visit—instead of a simple email or text—meant one of two things. Either he was lonely and wanted company or whatever he had to say was important enough it warranted the two of us sitting down to chat.

Both scenarios involved Calliope, of course. He'd said as much. Since she'd moved into Vesterville House with Thalia, that left my ex-husband to fend for himself. Since he was able to track down and apprehend despicable monsters for a living, you'd think he'd be capable of cooking and cleaning and finding his own socks. Not so much, at least when we were married. And when I'd bought my place and moved out, our daughter confirmed little had changed, except she was then doing for him what I'd been doing for him all along.

Which meant with both of us gone, he had to be at a loss. Not my problem, but a possible source of angst for him nonetheless that could have driven him to actually come to my house and see me in person.

Except, as I pulled up the long, tree-shadowed and hedged-in driveway past the stone wall and towering gate that was the entry to Thalia's family estate, I realized it was much more likely the other Calliope issue in question that had him ringing my doorbell at 6PM on a Thursday night.

You might think I was jumping to conclusions and perhaps I was. The fact my daughter and her girlfriend (literally, though they hadn't admitted it out loud yet) were living together and hadn't, as far as I knew, told anyone about their real feelings for one another, didn't mean Trent hadn't noticed. He was, after all, a profiler and incredibly intuitive when he wanted to be. Which was never, with me, though often enough with Calliope when she was growing up, she complained about failing to get away with anything.

So, if he had sorted out their relationship,

okay then. Not that it was a problem if he figured it out like I had. Unless.

Unless he was judging them for it. *Then* we'd have a problem.

But surely, I was overreacting. I pulled up to the top of the circular drive and parked, waiting for the girls to emerge, scowling out into the early evening spring sunshine like it didn't exist and could do nothing to warm the coldness engulfing me, my hands clenching on the steering wheel while I fought off the urge to text Trent what I thought of his reaction to our daughter finding love and happiness.

Saved by the appearance of said daughter and the other young woman in question who bounded out the front doors of Vesterville House, smiling and chattering while holding hands, the sight of tall, elderly Lloyd Mitchem, the family butler, waving at me from just inside before he closed the way behind him.

I just managed to smother the need to use that same expression on Trent with a firm pillow when Calliope pulled open the front passenger door and hopped in, her round cheeks pink, hazel eyes sparkling, those unruly dark curls of hers so like her father I had to remind myself to breathe. While she had his stocky build and facial features, she had my spirit, thank goodness, and when she leaned in to hug me, I returned her embrace with a tight squeeze and whispered, "Love you, kiddo."

Thalia, meanwhile, had made herself comfortable in the back seat behind Calliope, leaning in herself to kiss my cheek when I released Daughter #1 and offered an awkward hug thanks to the arrangement for Daughter #2. Her own blue eyes had that same glint of happiness, pale skin and long, fine blonde hair such a contrast to Calliope the pair looked like opposites in many ways. But though the Vesterville mistress, at a mere twenty-two, was tall and lean to the point of high-metabolism emaciation to my biological daughter's 5'2" athletic build, there was something utterly right about the two of them I guessed had a lot to do with the fact they'd been best friends long before this new evolution in their relationship.

"Sorry I'm late," I said. Almost told them why. Shrugged, smiled. "Hungry?" I didn't like withholding anything from my daughter, but as I drove off toward town, I reassured myself any conversation I had with Calliope and Thalia about Trent would happen after I spoke to him bluntly and directly about what his problem was.

Okay, Persephone. Big breath. Because that had to wait, too, until I actually knew what he wanted in the first place.

Instead of letting it trouble me further, I sank deeper into my seat and let the happy chatter from the girls lighten my mood. They shared their day (Calliope rambling on about things I'd forgotten the moment she stream-of-consciousnessed (no judging, that's a word now) into the next item while Thalia murmured her input in between her girlfriend's breaths) while I chose to set aside my fear I'd be murdering my ex-husband for daring to be a jerk about who my daughter chose to love.

So, not over it then. Awesome.

By the time we parked across the street from our destination, I'd calmed enough I enjoyed looping my arm through Calliope's, Thalia on her other side, the three of us joining fellow patrons who'd come to the grand re-opening of our favorite diner. I grinned at the flashing sign overhead, my friend, Ingrid Lowe, going with all layers of blues to complement the new name she'd chosen, sign's logo repeated in colorful relief on the front door as I reached for the handle and pulled open the entry to The Blueberry Grill.

Instant noise greeted us, though it wasn't nearly as packed as I'd expected. There was even a booth left in the back which Calliope squealed over and rushed to occupy, sliding across the navy vinyl seat to the window filling the whole front of the diner with the light of the day, golden sunset still an hour or so away, mingling with the retro fixture's incandescent bulb overhead, the shiny blue table-top lacquered over a sparkly inlay. I waved at Ingrid whose visibly weary face lit up at the sight of me, the short, petite woman hustling toward us in her blue t-shirt and matching apron, pausing a moment to chat with another group before heading our way again.

The long, narrow diner with its classic counter and bar behind, the kitchen on the other side of the swinging door with its large, round window had the same layout but a brand-new feel from the rather tired and dingy state of affairs that the last owners left it in. Mind you, I hardly blamed Margaret and Martin Offers, since the pair of them opened this place more than fifty years ago, working tirelessly, sometimes just the two of them, to keep the business afloat. They might have failed to upkeep the décor, but they knew how to cook and serve. Which meant Ingrid had big shoes to fill.

"Seph!" Ingrid landed at last, blowing Callie a kiss, giving Thalia a soft squeeze to her shoulder. "Thank you so much for coming." It was obvious to me my friend's state bordered on the frantic, her hands shaking just enough as adrenaline kept her going and likely little else aside from enough caffeine to sink a battleship, knowing her. "What do you think?" Her pause, her tension, the ache in her eyes had me instantly gushing.

"Gorgeous," I said, while Calliope sang, "Love it!" and Thalia murmured, "It's so beautiful, Ingrid."

She blew out a loud puff of air, sagging in what looked like relief, leaning in with her voice at a conspiratorial tone I was sure they heard throughout the whole diner. "It's so hard to know," she said. "There's been no time, and everything was running behind. Three weeks! I wanted to be open Monday." There'd been local grumbling about this favorite place closing for renos, but as far as I could tell, it was worth it. "I had to finish the menu on the fly, and I can't reach Martin to get the apple pie recipe he promised me, so I had to start from scratch." She eye-rolled, her whole being vibrating. "They just had to run off to Mexico, didn't they?"

Considering they'd been planning their first real vacation since their oldest son went to college… I hardly blamed them but didn't say so to Ingrid. Not that I had time to interrupt, her jitters carrying her onward in conversation without needing any kind of prompting.

"Here's the new menu." She whipped three out from inside her apron's pocket, the long, slim laminated sheets landing with a slap on the sparkly table. "I'll be bringing around a selection tonight, no orders, but you can at least see what will be available starting tomorrow."

She left then in a bustle while I smiled after her, happy for her but so very grateful it was her and not me. Looked up to see Thalia staring into Callie's eyes and vice versa. Almost put my foot in my mouth because, quite frankly, they just had to come out and say it already before I did and ruined their moment.

It comforted me, though, seeing them look at one another like that. Sure, the worry remained they'd outgrow one another someday, of course. But that was the nature of some relationships. Who knew? They might be the lucky ones who spent the rest of their lives together. No, my real worry had been more so the fact they chose to live in the family estate. Not that Vesterville House really had a cursed soul or anything. Maybe. Possibly. I knew better, of course. On the other hand, it was impossible to just set aside the fact the Vesterville family had seen their share of tragedy, more than their share, to be honest, and that the lingering darkness in that place felt like it had a life of its own.

Still, it was lovely to see Thalia so relaxed and happy, far more than she'd been since her parents were murdered almost four years ago now. And Calliope, while always an exuberant and outgoing young woman, had a maturity to her I was only just noticing, without any limitations added to her zest for life.

They must have felt me staring because they both looked at me suddenly, as one, forcing me to clear my throat and look away with a fake smile, handing out the menus like I wasn't caught intruding on a private moment between them.

Argh. Why wouldn't they just freaking tell me already?

"Diner breakfast!" Calliope grinned at me. "She kept the diner breakfast." It was our favorite and we split one every Sunday we could fit it in. Three eggs, tons of bacon, far more toast that was good for my hips, hash browns crisp from the fryer and endless coffee and homemade strawberry jam. Reading the listing, remembering the tastes, had me almost drooling.

The rest of the breakfast and lunch menu seemed rather untouched, old favorites returning which would make the regulars happy. But her dinner menu with homemade pasta and a charcuterie board that sounded divine along with a licensed bar—the original never had alcohol—had me pondering inviting some girlfriends out for a gab session, snacks and too much gin.

Just kidding. There was no such thing as too much gin. Speaking of which, I nodded to the attractive young woman who came toward us with a notepad in hand, anticipating one drink, at least, before the food came out.

At the exact moment he turned on his favorite stool and scowled at her, sticking his long legs out far enough she almost tripped.

"I hate all of it," Big Dan Adams said so loudly the whole place went silent. "Way to go, Ingrid, for ruining the best diner in Wallace."

CHAPTER THREE

Honestly, I was so surprised to find Big Dan there I hadn't even looked for him, the counter fixture and general pain in everyone's butt usually slurping coffee and yelling out life advice to other patrons the most vocal of all who protested (okay, the only one who came out and said it) the renovations, swearing he'd never set foot in Margaret's Kitchen again.

Apparently, he'd decided ruining Ingrid's night had far more impact attached to making himself scarce.

"Dad." Like clockwork, his son, Billy, spoke up then, the leaner, shorter and less oppressive version of the towering, big-bellied and opinionated elder of the two did his best to try to silence his father, but with about the same success as he usually did. Which meant none bordering on inspiring Big Dan to make himself more of a nuisance if at all possible.

"There was nothing wrong with the way things were," he said, rumbling voice just this side of a bellow, the occupants of the diner studiously ignoring him almost to a fault, though I found my earlier irritation at Trent had transferred quite smoothly to the noisy, belligerent middle-aged cis white guy and his patriarchal privilege sitting almost across from me.

The young waitress did her best to avoid him, dark cheeks tinted with a deep blush, nearly black eyes rimmed with moisture as she offered me a trembling smile in an attempt to push past the fact Big Dan had likely been at her more than just this once and she was nearing the edge of her patience.

"Are you okay?" I smiled back, sympathy and support in my expression, both of my girls leaning in with their own concerned looks because they had huge hearts, that pair, and didn't hesitate to support another woman in need.

"I'm fine, thank you," she answered in a small voice. "Is he always so…?"

I shot him a quelling look over her shoulder while he flipped me a rather rude hand gesture that was about to win him a tongue lashing from his (not so) friendly neighborhood holistic therapist. "Yes," I said, disdain at full. "Unfortunately." Rather than stoop to his level, I chose to focus on the young woman in front of me. "I'm Persephone Pringle. I don't think I've seen you in Wallace before."

She seemed startled I introduced myself, glanced at the girls in turn before dimpling a lovely white smile against her warm brown cheeks. "Gabriella," she said, with just a hint of a Latino accent. "Gabriella Torres. I'm here from… Portland."

Why the hesitation? Not that it mattered, but she seemed nervous all over again, swallowed while Calliope and Thalia both said hello, giving their names while she bobbed nods that had her high-tied ponytail of thick, black hair bouncing.

I had to repeat my drink order twice—who knew gin and cranberry on ice in a short glass with no lime or straw was a complicated thing to remember?—though the girls had better luck with their milkshakes, vanilla for Thalia and chocolate (with extra fudge) for Calliope fairly straightforward. Which had me guessing part of Gabriella's nervousness and upset likely had to do as much with Big Dan's yelling as it did her inexperience at the job.

As she turned, now smiling and much more

at ease, I wasn't fast enough to keep Dan from reaching out and snatching her order pad from her hands. Okay, dude, that was borderline assault and would get him more than a talking to once our fourth arrived, (you think I'd be out with two twentysomethings with no backup?) hopefully any second now.

Gabriella stopped, eyes huge, clearly not knowing what to do. Before I could surge out of my seat and tear him a new one for tormenting the girl, the childish piece of work laughing as he tossed her notebook to the floor and put his foot on it, another new face intruded, this time from behind the counter.

The short, stocky but incredibly muscular man with more tattoos than I had (that was saying something) didn't seem to care he was covered in flour and other food remnants, nor did he appear reluctant to hide the fact if he reached Big Dan in the next two seconds, he was probably going to punch the loudmouth in the face.

My money was on who had to be Ingrid's cook, but I never got to make the bet. Gabriella stopped him with a touch on his truly impressive bicep.

"It's okay, Saucy," she said in a small voice.

"It's *not*." He bent and grabbed the notebook out from under Big Dan's shoe with a hearty shove to the older man's toes, Dan grunting at the contact, his stool turning him into the next patron before he could stop himself. When he righted his seat, he was scowling instead of that sickening smirk he always wore, but Saucy was still talking. "You don't like The Blueberry Grill? Then get *out*." His slurring and slightly accented words made him hard to make out at first. He gestured at the door while the diner again fell silent, even Ingrid staring open-mouthed from the cash register. "There are other joints in town where talkback rules, but this ain't one of them."

Well now. Good for Saucy.

Big Dan wasn't to be outdone, however, bluster rising as he puffed up his chest, massive belly jiggling over his lap, florid cheeks flushing darker as his piggy eyes narrowed, sweat breaking out into the thinning front of his hairline.

"I'm a paying customer," he snapped. "You can't kick me out. I've supported this diner for years. Margaret and Martin always welcomed me and I'm not leaving."

"You missed my point," Saucy shot back, my mind getting used to his street-talk and translating some of the words, "Margaret and Martin ain't here no more. This here is Ingrid's place now." She approached at a trot, her expression a mix of horror and amusement I could feel in the pit of my stomach. On the one hand, this was her first night and Dan's level of conflict could mean people didn't come back. On the other, I'd never seen anyone put the loudmouth complainer—oh, you bet he complained to everyone, all the time—in his place.

Saucy looked like he had more to say, but Ingrid was faster, grabbing his arm and tugging on him, dragging him back behind the counter and to the kitchen door while someone laughed. It was a low and mocking sound, unexpected in the quiet, drawing my attention to the young, handsome man at the end of the counter, his suit jacket open, what looked like a silk shirt beneath black to match his two-piece, open to the third button. There was no way he was any kind of businessman, however, not with that excessively styled hair and one-day scruff and rakish attitude that screamed rich boy slumming. But I'd never seen him before and caught myself glancing at Thalia to see if she recognized him while he stopped his cynical chuckle and spoke.

"I had no idea there would be such lovely entertainment," he said. "Is this little town always so amusing?"

Big Dan spun toward him with a heavy

scowl, jowls spreading out as he lowered his head in a bull-like show of aggression. "Mind your own business."

"No," the young man said then, toying with a spoon that he set down suddenly, decisively, the rattling sound reaching everyone in the room. "I don't think I will." He gestured to the door. "As the rather succinct staff member said, there are other establishments in town. Perhaps you'd be happier at one of them. We'd all certainly be delighted if you decided to relocate." He winked at me. "All in favor?"

I almost applauded. Held off, only because, in the stillness that followed, the doorbells jangled and the force of nature I'd been waiting to sweep in and bring order to this one-horse diner strode in.

Sheriff Cherise King had perfect timing, as usual, towering and Amazonian physique out of uniform at the moment, though she looked far more dangerous in dark jeans and a dress jacket over a dark blue button-up with her cowboy boots thudding on the floor and that near buzz-cut of hers doing nothing to hide her stunning face, deep skin shining, black eyes taking in the scene as if she knew exactly what she was walking into.

I had no idea what it was like to grow up in Chicago or to rise in ranks in that police department to become head of a homicide squad, but whatever was required for such a position, Cherise had it and so much more.

Dan took one look at her and turned slowly toward the counter, sullen pout the kind of petulance I expected from a toddler who knew his tantrum wasn't going to get him anything no matter how hard he tried.

My shero to the rescue.

CHAPTER FOUR

There was no way the sheriff could have known Dan was making trouble. She'd entered during the looming and uncomfortable silence, without evidence of specific persons involved, her arrival triggering a shift in the feel of the place, from dread and anticipation of escalating conflict to a wash of relief and a rise in anticipation that sent goosebumps up my arms. As though, to a patron, we knew the calvary had arrived and we were safe at last.

Did Cherise know the impact she had on people around her? There had been some pushback when she'd been hired rather than going through an election process, the sheriff's position here in Wallace handled through town council instead. Not because of her race or skin tone or the fact she was from Chicago. Our last sheriff had been black, but he was local and, let's be frank about the real reason for hesitation, a man. But Cherise had shown in the last year and a half since she'd taken over law enforcement in our town and surrounds just how lucky we were to have her, with the best crime-solving rate in the state, so impressive the state police even consulted with her from time to time, while her new programs and education for her deputies lowered the crime rate significantly.

Aside from the two murders in the last year, that was. Not my fault, despite the fact I'd been involved in both to some degree. And since both had been solved, that meant even more accolades and trust for the equally impressive visually as she was intelligently sheriff of Wallace.

Call it intuition or the fact she knew his penchant for stirring things up just for fun, Cherise paused next to Big Dan who stared down at his coffee mug, red-faced and refusing to look up while she smiled a pleasant, professional smile and tapped the counter next to him with one index finger.

"Dan," she said. "Hope you're having a good evening. And that you're letting these folks have one, too."

He grunted something I didn't catch before

Billy spoke up in a rush.

"He'll behave himself, Sheriff King," he said, prodding his father. "We don't want any trouble for Ingrid."

Cherise nodded, still smiling. "Let's just be sure that's the case, shall we? Gentlemen." She pivoted on her boot, turning toward our booth, grin broadening into a greeting. I felt the tension snap, my shoulders loosening when the tall sheriff slipped in next to Thalia across from me. "I take it that I missed out on all the excitement?" She kept her voice low, but the chatter in the place had fired up again, so it was doubtful anyone would have heard her.

I shrugged, grinned, Gabriella delivering our order, my glass of gin a welcome addition while the girls helped themselves to their shakes, old enough to drink but neither choosing to do so. Cherise, for her part, asked for a beer, the young waitress flashing me a smile that looked like gratitude as she hustled off again, this time without interference from Dan.

"You could say that." I tipped my glass to her. "Funny how trouble crawls into a hole and hides when Sheriff King shows up."

She chuckled at that. "I wish," she said, shaking her head, thick lashes rimming her dark eyes making me jealous as always. But there was a troubled look there that bothered me, as though she had more to say.

Ingrid appeared at our booth before I could respond or try to lure the details out of Cherise, the still-vibrating new owner almost in tears as she clasped the sheriff's hand. "Thank you," she said, just above a whisper. "I tried to tell him to leave earlier, but he's such a bully." She didn't have to name names for us to know who she meant.

"You have the right to ban him, Ingrid," Cherise said, serious now, her protector of all things innocent persona like a shield wall around her and engulfing Ingrid at the same time. "If you need help doing so, let me know." The sheriff's gaze flickered sideways to where the man in question perched on his stool, son whispering hastily and what looked like with real anxiety to his father. Billy appeared worried enough as his own eyes landed on Cherise while he hissed whatever warning or coercion he used on Big Dan, so it was obvious to me the young man knew his father walked thin ice.

Ingrid relaxed just a little, wiping quickly at her eyes when she released Cherise's hand, nodding. "Thank you," she said again. "I might take you up on that." And scurried away once more, Gabriella delivering the sheriff's beer at the same moment.

"Some people," Cherise said then in a low and angry voice that hummed between us like a threat, "should learn that stirring up mischief to satisfy their inner demons means they stop being welcome in this town."

"Has Dan been an issue lately?" I forced myself to focus on her rather than the pair at the counter, Billy still talking fast while Big Dan's stool swished back and forth just a little, the lumbering irritant in plaid and a jean jacket clearly fighting the urge to blow up again.

Cherise didn't confirm or deny until after she'd had a long pull on her beer. "Let's just say he hasn't taken Little Dan's passing very well." Right, his namesake and Billy's older brother. He'd died tragically a year ago, in Bangor, murdered in a mugging or something. "Grief does things to people." She'd softened somewhat, but I could tell if push came to standing up for Wallace, Cherise was the perfect woman for the job.

I looked up when the other young waitress hurried toward us, laying out a tray of samples of food for us to try. The lightened atmosphere and delicious smells—not to mention the softening inside from the hit of gin—had me relaxing somewhat, though the sight of Saucy the cook peeking out of the kitchen, gaze directed at Cherise before he flinched and disappeared again had me wondering. Well, with a nickname like Saucy, maybe he had a few things in his past he'd rather the police didn't know about.

And, more likely, I'd imagined it and really needed to mind my business rather than stir up my own brand of trouble for my sheriff friend.

The evening marched on, my second and last gin of the evening sending me to the ladies' room, still thinking about the delicious treats Ingrid passed out with liberal generosity for us to try. I loved the idea of a sampler board, flat cost for a variety of items rather than having to settle for one particular dish, always a problem when I went out to eat. How was I supposed to choose? This way I didn't have to, and I had a feeling Ingrid's idea would draw in a lot of people for the same reason.

I knew I'd be back, and not just because she was a friend. Whether Saucy was someone unsavory or not, the man could cook.

I was exiting the bathroom, sliding past two chattering women who both nodded hello when I noted a young black man in a yellow hoody and dark jeans speaking with the wealthy young man from the end of the diner. They stood near the entrance to the men's room, the newcomer's dark face intent and visibly upset, the rich kid's smirk insulting even without context. One of my bracelets caught on the door handle, forcing me to pause, which gave me a moment to eavesdrop whether I wanted to or not.

"I told you, Rider," yellow hoody said. "Wallace is *my* digs. You're not welcome here."

"And *I* told *you*," the one he'd called Rider said, "the likes of *you*," he jabbed the younger man in the chest with one index finger, "doesn't get to tell *me*," another jab, "where I'm allowed to do business. Really, Checks. You're out of your league, kid. Get lost." Rider pushed past him and by me like I didn't exist, heading for the counter again and his seat. The young man he'd called Checks met my eyes briefly, his startlingly amber ones against the depth of his skin tone making me stare. He dropped his gaze on the way by, hands stuffed into the front pocket of his hoody, scowling as he went.

When I returned to our table, it was to Cherise watching Checks go, the young man ignoring her wave of hello on the way by, my sheriff friend's intense stare when she turned slowly in her seat to observe his exit no less so when he finally walked out through the glass door to the rattle of bells and refocused on me.

"I take it you know Checks," I said.

Cherise's eyebrows arched while the girls

ignored us, their conversation carrying on like the sheriff and I didn't exist. "I do," she said. "How do you?"

"I get around," I said like that was actually a thing as Cherise snorted. "Overheard him talking to the overdressed young man at the counter." The sheriff's gaze found Rider, returned to me. "Something about business and territory."

She finished her second beer, shoved the bottle aside, sighed. "Thanks for the heads up," she said. "No rest for the wicked." Cherise planted both hands on the tabletop, clearly ready to rise and, I could only guess, have a chat with the well-dressed and arrogant young man.

Didn't get to, though. Because for whatever reason that could possibly possess someone like him—I'm sure I'd never know even with hours of billable sessions to unravel his hate—Big Dan chose that moment to make a spectacle of himself, Cherise or no Cherise.

With a heavy thud of a fist landing on the counter that actually rattled the contents in front of him, Big Dan stood, visibly swaying and likely with too much beer in his belly if the bottles in front of him told the story (why Ingrid would keep serving him I had no idea). "I want another beer!"

Ah, so she'd cut him off then. Shouldn't have given him any in the first place, as far as I was concerned, but it wasn't my diner.

Cherise was on her feet and beside Dan, his few inches in height difference and bulky weight dominance doing nothing to intimidate her. She was in his space and speaking softly to him even before his commanding bellow's echo had faded, the sheriff gesturing at Billy who stood so fast he stumbled, grabbing his father's arm and leading him out, Cherise following, Big Dan glaring back at her over his shoulder. Whatever it was the sheriff said to him, he complied, looking rebellious but defeated this time at least.

I didn't expect the round of applause that chased Dan out, Cherise pausing as he slammed his way through the glass door and out into the street, the clapping turning into cheering and whistling that she clearly couldn't ignore. With a short nod and a wave for the crowd and then me and the girls she exited the diner to continuing shouts of appreciation while I grinned and shook my head at her celebrity moment.

Best sheriff *ever*.

CHAPTER FIVE

With Cherise gone, the evening wrapping up, I took notice of how overwhelmed and weary Ingrid looked and made a decision while the slowly departing patrons waved to her and left, leaving her with a giant mess and two stressed waitresses who looked about to drop where they stood.

"I'll be right back, girls." I slid out of the booth, Calliope and Thalia barely noticing me leaving, and headed for the counter. Ingrid had disappeared back into the kitchen and while I hadn't been invited, I felt compelled to reach out and make an offer of assistance.

Which had me slipping through the kitchen door and into the back of the diner where the renovations had clearly stopped. Then again, the fresh coat of white paint and stainless-steel appliances looked new enough, but any kind of fancy update had been set aside for a simple refresh as far as I could tell, and fair enough. Not like most patrons would get a look back here anyway.

I was surprised when I found the kitchen empty, dishes piled in the large double sinks, Saucy missing, the back door to the alley outside partially open. I spotted the cook in question talking with a familiar young man, his yellow hoody unmistakable, Checks with his head down, talking fast.

As tempting as it was to poke my nose outside and try to hear what they were talking about, I wasn't fast enough. Gabriella almost ran right into me when I realized I'd stopped in the worst place possible, the young woman dropping a tray of plates and shattering them on the floor thanks to my presence and interference. Before I could apologize, wincing at my clumsiness, she burst into tears.

A hug and some comforting murmurings seemed to help calm her. When she pulled back from the embrace I instantly offered, Gabriella hiccupped through her remaining tears.

"I'm so sorry," she said. "I'm terrible at this."

"You're not," I said, "and it's not your fault. Let me help you clean up." Her relief and gratitude had me scrambling deeper into the kitchen in search of a broom and dustpan, the sound of her scooping up broken ceramic only increasing my guilt. I'd be offering to pay for the damage as soon as I finished sorting out the mess.

A large, metal door with the long black handle stood partially ajar, the walk-in freezer suddenly slammed shut as Ingrid emerged, leaning her back against it, a terrified look on her face. Her reaction had me so startled I stared at her a long moment while she stared back, before she pushed herself forward, that horror I'd seen shifting into a stammering attempt at welcome.

"I'm looking for a broom," I said. "I made a mess."

Ingrid rubbed her hands on her apron over and over again, her nervous energy only more visible when she tried to smile, failed, anxiety simmering in her eyes. "It's fine," she said, reaching out and grabbing me, pushing me toward the kitchen door. "It's all fine. I can handle it. Thank you, Seph, it's fine!"

By the time she repeated herself for the third time, I was through the swinging door past Gabriella and into the diner proper once again, Ingrid spinning the moment I was out of her kitchen and returning to the back, leaving me confused and concerned and more than a little guilty.

I'd barely reached my seat when Ingrid reemerged, the last of the patrons—us included—gathering our things, the girls ready to go when I returned. I paused to say goodnight, but Ingrid avoided me, hugging both Calliope and Thalia who gushed their thanks, clueless, the two of them, while all I got was a wave.

Well now. That was a little rude but considering I'd made a mess while trying to help, I suppose I earned a bit of distance. Still, it was hard not to worry about Ingrid and whatever it was she'd been dealing with when my interference only added to her concerns. While perplexing, if she didn't want my help, I wasn't going to force it on her.

I dropped the girls off at Vesterville House around 10PM, knowing it was a terrible idea but stopping Calliope before she got out, that much of my own mystery in my power to possibly solve. After all, if I was jumping to conclusions about Trent, my daughter might be able to clear it up.

"Any idea why your father might want to talk to me?" I waited for a reaction that could give me an in for my own line of questions. Was I reading something into her hesitation that wasn't there? Apparently, because a moment later Calliope just frowned and shook her head.

"No clue," she said, eyes wide, innocent. So, either she was getting very good at lying to me—I hoped not but she was a smart girl raised by a therapist and a profiler, after all—or she was telling me the truth and he was a jerk. Please let it not be the former. I'd raised her to be honest with herself and those around her, and the idea she was lying to me for any reason sat very heavily on me. "Everything okay?"

"I'm sure," I said, kissing her cheek, choosing not to press the issue. I decided to trust her instead. "Night, sweetie."

"Night, Mom." She hesitated one moment, leading me to believe yet again there might be something, or that she even could be on the brink of finally coming out to me. But the instant passed, and she instead waved and slammed the door, she and Thalia hand in hand on their way up the steps.

Maybe she thought I already knew and didn't need to tell me. There was that.

Yeah. Right.

I pulled into my driveway fifteen minutes later, Belladonna meeting me at the door with a soft chirped question.

"It was okay," I said, scooping her into my arms. "An evening full of questions and drama, what else is new?" She purred, rubbing her furry face against my cheek. "Like you really care. Want a snack before bed, sweet girl?"

Despite my best intentions and a few breathing exercises to still my mind and thoughts, it was a restless night that ended with me up earlier than I intended, Belladonna fed and a couple of hours free before my only Friday client. While I had contemplated just texting Trent and forcing him to tell me his issues over messages so I wouldn't be in his proximity if I did feel stabby over his reason for this conversation, I knew from years of experience if he wanted a face-to-face no amount of demanding or cajoling or asking would make him tell me anything he didn't want to say.

Already frustrated by lack of sleep and spinning scenarios I had no real reason to allow space in my head without corroboration, I headed out, knowing he'd be in the office early (wouldn't matter what day of the week, Trent worked every day) and decided to get this over with before it could ruin the rest of my day.

I had to take Main Street, which had me driving past The Blueberry Grill and, with a hankering for a coffee and wanting to check in on Ingrid also adding layers to the complicated conflicts I juggled since last night, I pulled into an empty spot outside and headed through the glass doors to a full and bustling breakfast crowd. The scent of java and eggs mixed with toast and fried yumminess had my stomach growling in a crawling reminder I'd skipped breakfast. I waved at Gabriella who served two giant plates to a booth at the back. She waved back but didn't approach, already skipping to the next booth with her tray tucked under her arm and her notepad out.

There was no sign of any other staff out front and enough disgruntled expressions, murmurs from the table next to me about slow service, I knew Ingrid was in trouble if she didn't pick up the pace. At least there was no sign of Big Dan, so whatever Cherise said to him last night must have gotten through or he'd be perched like a permanent fixture on his stool and remained there all day like usual.

Small miracles, but no Ingrid and a gathering of hungry folks who, if unhappy, could ruin her before she had a chance to really shine. Which had me, yet again, ducking into the kitchen despite myself, though I made sure to get out of the way of the door as I entered.

"Ingrid?" No sign of Saucy, the cook, though again the back door stood partially open so he could have been taking a quick break. Hardly the time for it, as far as I was concerned, now worried Ingrid might have bitten off more than she could chew (no pun intended) if she was short-staffed and packed like this.

This time when I noted the walk-in door was open, I went right to it, the memory of Ingrid's terror from the night before piquing my curiosity enough I had to know what it was that triggered such a horrified reaction.

I paused just inside the chilly space, right behind the frozen (again, no pun meant, I swear) form of Ingrid, her back to me, hands clenched into fists at her sides, immobile and silent. I reached out to her, my anxiety for her rising, worried she'd snapped maybe, or was having a silent meltdown, circling her a little, hand on her shoulder.

She didn't move, still staring, the barest trembling felt under my fingers. While I turned to seek out what had her in such a state.

Realized while he might not be able to cause trouble any longer, Big Dan had really outdone himself this time. Dead, slumped and staring at the both of us, frozen rather stiff with his mouth hanging open in a slack expression of pain, the resident troublemaker certainly knew how to make an exit.

CHAPTER SIX

Waiting to talk to Cherise about a dead body seemed to be a habit I'd been forming, though to be fair I'd been the second person to walk in on Big Dan's last effort to ruin someone's continuing existence while he got to be the star of the show. That said individual had the sheriff's focus and attention while I stood aside and waited my turn, the hustling and very busy diner now closed and shuttered to the group of unhappy customers the deputies had escorted off the premises without breakfast.

I just hoped their terrible experience didn't bode badly for Ingrid's future success. Mind you, having a dead body turn up in one's establishment the day after opening didn't really lend itself to a positive outlook, but considering this particular corpse always brought bad news with him, at least Ingrid knew once this was over, he'd no longer be a source of conflict for her or her staff.

Silver linings, right?

Then again, I couldn't help the momentary—just for the briefest of guilty seconds, I swear—worry maybe my friend, frustrated and furious and at her wit's end, had taken matters into her own hands at some point last night, perhaps if Big Dan had made his presence known after closing and she'd been offered no choice in the matter, was Ingrid capable of the obvious?

I couldn't bring myself to believe that, though her horrified expression came back to me from the night before, her slamming of the walk-in's door, the way she'd practically thrown me out of the diner just a short time after Cherise escorted the still irritable and likely belligerent Big Dan from the Grill all lent itself to the slim but real possibility Ingrid may have reacted in a way that ended in the man's demise.

Not that I believed she was capable of murdering anyone. Accidental death? Passion-driven manslaughter? Well, I'd been a therapist and student of human nature long enough to know when pushed to their limits, homo sapiens, even the kindest of us, were capable of amazing feats (and some of them awful, too) when the situation made other options impossible.

Cherise finally stepped away from Ingrid after a soft squeeze to her shoulder, the diner owner turning and heading for a stool where she planted herself and buried her face in her hands. Gabriella stood off to one side, weeping and speaking to a deputy while the sheriff got around to me.

Okay, not her fault my morning was now shot after a terrible night's sleep and yet another corpse to add to my collection. But it was that sort of ridiculous mental gymnastics that led me to thinking I was now cursed with the duty of uncovering every dead person and their means of exodus from this world Wallace would have to offer from now on.

Cherise had her cop face on and, though it was as kind and confident as ever, it still gave me more fuel for my irritated fire. "I have no idea why this keeps happening," I said.

She laughed at that, soft and low, my friend showing through the law enforcement façade while she offered me that same gentle shoulder squeeze she'd just given to Ingrid. "What can you tell me, Seph?"

I filled her in with dutiful attention to detail

while flinching a bit at feeling like a traitor since I'd only a few months before held back the truth of another murderer's identity to protect loved ones from repercussions. Lying to Cherise wasn't something I took lightly, and I know I now overcompensated. Though telling her about Ingrid's reaction to the contents of the walk-in last night wasn't an overreaction if her eyebrow rises and piqued interest meant anything.

I finished with Saucy talking outside with Checks the night before as an afterthought, then the obvious. "There's no sign of the cook," I said. "The back door was open, and he was gone when I arrived. If he's involved somehow, he might have run."

"No sign of Billy Abrams either," Cherise said, quiet enough for just us as she closed her notebook and tucked it and her pen away. "I have deputies looking. But meanwhile, I have to look into Ingrid." She glanced over her shoulder, the diner owner now more composed but staring and slack-lipped, in visible shock. "I know you two are friends, Seph. Can you talk to her with me?" I hesitated, not because I didn't want to help but because I had to know if she was asking me as a friend and not a therapist. Cherise cleared that up with her next words. "The Wallace Sheriff's

Department officially requests professional assistance." That answered that and had me breathing a bit easier because not only was it now an official opportunity, I could treat it with a more detached and therapeutic approach than waffling between work and friendship. While it might seem to you I'd have been happier to act out of the latter, drawing on my work gave me a level of confidence I wouldn't make a mess of Cherise's investigation in case a lawyer later asked why I was involved.

Amazing what you need to consider when dead bodies show up out of the blue.

Cherise, meanwhile, carried on. "She's a bit incoherent at the moment and I need the full story. Besides, you've been down this road before, so consider yourself the resident therapist, okay? I'd like to know I can call you in on cases without having to worry about red tape."

I nodded immediately, joining her without hestitation, wondering if I'd just made a terrible decision making crimefighting a part of my practice but secretly thrilled knowing Cherise trusted me that much.

Make no mistake, Trent would never have broached such an idea and the truth of that hurt more than I wanted to admit.

The moment I reached Ingrid she snapped out of her daze, eyes glazed but speaking clearly when she grasped for me and held onto my hand like a lifeline. "This is terrible," she said, voice cracking but perfectly audible. "How did he end up in my walk-in like that?" As though she struggled to comprehend that was the exact reason Cherise and I were there. Which meant her mind was still jumbled and if she had something to do with his death it would be relatively easy to get her to talk about it. But the fact she opened with that question, the delivery authentic, I felt confident setting aside the momentary doubt I'd had she may have had something to do with his end and instead focused on drawing out what she did know for sure.

"Ingrid," I said, "do you have cameras in the kitchen? Our outside in the alley?" That might answer everything for us.

She gaped at me, then shook her head. "It's a safe area," she said, sounding like she no longer believed that. "Margaret and Martin never had them. I was going to, the insurance company said it would lower my premiums." Trembling began in her hands, then her shoulders, more tears rising in her eyes. "The renovations were late, and I was already over budget, I thought I'd just wait and do it next month."

I caught movement, heard Cherise mutter to a deputy who came to her gesture, leaving Gabriella to answer her summons. "Check surrounding businesses for footage," she said while Ingrid went on, the deputy exiting through the back door, pushing it partially shut behind him.

"When can I open again?" Her desperate question was aimed at Cherise, not me, Ingrid now shaking so much the stool she sat on rattled. "I need to open, Sheriff King. I'm losing money every second I'm closed and if I can't open…" she fell silent suddenly, looking up at the ceiling over the sink for a moment. Odd. Her gaze snapped back to the sheriff who observed the same behavior but answered Ingrid without asking questions.

"I'm afraid you'll be closed at least a few days." The back door swung open again, Owen Graves stepping through, already dressed in his white coveralls and blue booties, the hood pulled up over his face, gloved hands placing his clear goggles as he entered. He waved to Cherise who pointed at the walk-in door, two EMTs following the young coroner/forensics expert/local mortician to examine and then recover the body.

"Ingrid," I distracted her from their arrival,

smiling kindly, holding her hand and speaking in a slow and measured way intended to gain and keep her attention. It worked, her bulging eyes fixed on me. "Can you tell us what happened?"

CHAPTER SEVEN

She shuddered all over, but it had the positive side effect of slowing her shivers to a faint tremble, Ingrid using her free hand to wipe a thin sheen of sweat from her upper lip and high forehead, speaking to me directly, as though Cherise wasn't watching and listening.

"It was so busy right from the moment I opened the door," she said, rather breathless. "Gabriella was late and the other girl, Tanya, didn't show up. Saucy was here, but he left an hour in without saying a word." She seemed flabbergasted by that. "I was running between helping Gabriella serve and making food," she faltered. Stopped. Looked down at the floor, tears dripping while she fought for air. I gently squeezed her hand, murmured comforting phrases to her until she caught herself again.

When she finally straightened, she wiped at her streaming eyes and nose with the corner of her apron. "I needed more hash browns from the walk-in." She choked, shook her head, her short hair bouncing, face deeply lined, dark circles now deep bruises under her puffy eyes, cheeks almost collapsing in on themselves as she sucked her lower lip to keep from sobbing again. "I have no idea how long I was standing there before you came in, Seph."

"What time was that?" Cherise's soft interruption had me turning to respond.

"About 8AM," I said, only remembering because I'd checked the clock in the car before getting out.

We all turned at a commotion coming from the walk-in door, the two EMTs grunting as they wheeled out the gurney. Not just because of its weight now laden down with the body of Big Dan Abrams, but the awkwardness of his positioning. They'd somehow hoisted his frozen body onto the surface, but since he was immobilized in the sitting position, getting him through the doorway was proving problematic, the body rocking so violently it almost tipped, my breath catching at the horrific image of him hitting the tile floor and shattering.

I knew it wasn't a real fear. Had dropped enough frozen meat over the years I knew better. Not that him bouncing was something to look forward to either, mind you. But at least there wouldn't be chunks and slivers of Big Dan to clean up like the broken ceramics from last night.

My brain was gross sometimes.

Owen emerged, stopping the EMTs who fought to strap down the man's massive girth before they managed to wrangle him onto his side. Facing us. Lovely, those filmed over eyes staring, mouth hanging open, hands on his chest, knees bent, a Big Dan popsicle. Another lovely mental image I could have done without and blamed on my overactive imagination while the EMTs finally managed to exit with one last bit of drama at the lip of the door to outside giving them a thudding and swaying pending overturn before they disappeared into the alley beyond.

Owen didn't seem all that concerned by the rather troublesome exit, joining us with a nod for Cherise and myself, launching into his reveal without consideration for the fact Ingrid was with us.

The kid was brilliant but not always smart if you know what I mean.

"Looks like a heart attack," he said. "Likely about eight hours ago." I counted back to midnight and TOD. "He's not quite frozen solid, so it shouldn't take too long for him to defrost." Dear heavens, really, Owen? Ingrid's shaking started up all over again, the insensitivity of Owen's rather blunt delivery clearly having an impact. "I checked the temp of the unit," he gestured back over his shoulder, "and it's set at -5, within standard."

"Fahrenheit, please, Owen," Cherise said.

"Right," he said. "That's what I get for going to college in Canada. Twenty-three, sheriff, and well within normal limits." He stripped off his gloves with snapping sounds, fisting them as he finished. "With his amount of body fat and what he was wearing," a jacket, right? He'd been wearing a jacket, flannel shirt over jeans, boots, all those details flashing in my mind along with the lingering stare of the dead I could do without, "he shouldn't have died from the cold. Unless he ran out of oxygen, which is possible, but I saw no signs of hypoxia. Still, carbon dioxide poisoning is really hard to nail down." He tossed his gloves into a plastic bag which he tucked into a pocket through a slit in the side of his coverall. "I do know he was alive when he went in, though, because there are signs on his hands and damage to one boot that matches a dent in the door near the handle he was trying to get out." Um, wow, Owen. Awful and really unnecessary, just laying it all out in clinical detachment like that. Not to him, apparently. "I'll know more when he's defrosted." With that, he turned and left, Cherise speaking up while I shook my head at his lack of social skills and made a note to have a little chat with the genius who gave no thought to people's feelings.

"What time did you leave last night, Ingrid?" Cherise was still gentle, but I knew that attitude wouldn't last forever, the diner owner now in another spiral I could feel in the shaking of her grasping hand. I needed to focus on the job she assigned me, not Owen's conversational habits.

"Ingrid," I said, "I left around 9:30PM with the girls, you remember?" She nodded to me, grasping onto my words with a panicked need to connect, staring in my eyes, her own lost. "You were closing."

"The last person left right after you," she said. "I sent the girls home an hour later after we cleaned up. Maybe 10:30PM?" She licked her lips, bobbing a nod at her own assessment. "I stayed behind for another half hour, I guess, did some paperwork, set up for this morning. I was home by just after 11PM." She pointed at the back door. "I remember it was about five after eleven because the news was on."

That sounded perfectly logical, and her voice was stronger, so I carried on. "Does anyone else have a set of keys to the diner?"

She shook her head immediately. "The guys said they'd make me some copies, but it was so busy they forgot."

"Guys?" That was all Cherise with such an excellent question. "What guys, Ingrid?"

She only glanced at the sheriff a moment, her horror returning, gaze flashing to me the next second. It was clear to me then she held herself together by believing I was the only one she needed to talk to. If that was the case, Cherise made the right call and I had to hand it to her for knowing so.

"The renovation company," she said. "TGM Properties. The foreman was going to take care of it."

"I'll need his full name and the contact information," Cherise said.

Ingrid slipped a hand into her apron and fished out a rumpled card, handed it over. Cherise offered it back, but the diner owner waved it off, suddenly sagging like she'd given up.

"Keep it," she whispered. "I don't need it anymore."

My phone buzzed, a call coming through at the worst possible time, and from someone I really didn't want to send to voicemail. But when I hesitated, Cherise gestured for me to answer.

"We're done here," she said. "For now. Ingrid, do you have someone who can take you home?"

I parted ways with the sheriff and diner owner to answer, Calliope's sweet voice rather hushed and reserved when I said hello.

"Hey, Mom," she said, inhaled a long breath, let it out in a huff. "I think I might know what Dad wants to talk to you about and I'm kind of angry about it." She had always been awesome about expressing her feelings, about being honest about them with me and not just because I was a therapist and encouraged it. My kid had a thing about truthfulness that I knew came far more from her FBI father than me.

"Okay, sweetie," I said. "Let's talk about it."

"Can we come by the house?" Ah, she and Thalia both, then? Or did she mean her father? "Thalia and I have something we need to tell you." Phew, not Trent. Was it wrong I was glad that was the case?

Avoidance, while not my norm, seemed to continue to be my go-to with my ex.

"I'm just heading home," I said. "Meet you at the house in ten?"

"Love you, Mom," she said ever-so-softly and hung up.

Why did those three simple words make me want to cry?

CHAPTER EIGHT

I made sure Ingrid had a deputy escort home before leaving myself, though Cherise seemed as concerned for her emotional state as I was, so I really didn't need to linger. Maybe it was a reactionary move on my part, some dread at what the girls had to say (if I was wrong about what I thought they planned to tell me) and what that implication meant for my ex-husband's continuing existence balanced against the expectation of relief they were going to finally come out to me all wrapped in worry they weren't and I'd have to play dumb while they dumped some other tragedy in my lap.

Oh, the cycle of dread and joy that was the human brain attempting to anticipate every happenstance. Such a treat.

I headed out the back door instead of going through the front, knowing the deputy on guard wouldn't mind unlocking it for me but wanting a peek at the alleyway despite the fact it wasn't my area of expertise. Cherise didn't comment, on the phone when I left with a wave, stepping out into the narrow space between buildings. I paused to look at the lock, noting it was new, no sign of anyone tampering with it or trying to force it. Not that I was an expert, mind you, and a skilled lock picker might be able to do the deed. But the deadbolt lock on top was another story. Which meant whatever happened to Big Dan, keys were used.

The question remained—who had them and if the construction foreman failed to make a set as he told Ingrid, how did Dan get in?

A dark blue dumpster stood against the restaurant's back wall, the lid up, a stack of discarded construction materials next to it. I caught sight of a vinyl corrugated sign tucked behind the waste bin and tugged it out, TGM Properties and their logo dominating the large white rectangle while a handful of other, smaller logos circled it, likely all subcontractors to the main company. For whatever reason, Ingrid had wasted no time discarding the advertising for the reno outfit along with whatever materials the workers left behind.

With nothing else of note popping up to wave a flag, I realized how silly my choice was, circling out of the end of the alley toward the front of the diner while shaking my head at myself. What I thought I'd uncover when a trained professional like Cherise and her deputies wouldn't was beyond me, which meant I was more tired than I was willing to admit and delaying again.

The moment I stepped out from the alley to the main sidewalk, another opportunity to dodge talking to my daughter presented, though this one was more than valid. I crossed the street in a hurry, waving to a car that slowed so I could jaywalk, barely acknowledging the driver's unhappiness out of concern for the more obvious display going on at the parking meter kitty-corner to The Blueberry Grill.

Billy Abrams stood with his hands in both pockets of his jeans, weeping openly, hazel eyes locked on the front door of the diner, sniffling over and over again as he swayed but made no move to run when I joined him. He didn't even glance my way, denim jacket and flannel shirt under his dark blue Wallace High sweatshirt a match for his father's, down to his work boots. I guess Big Dan taught his boys his fashion sense, but not his attitude, the young man's grief seemingly a far cry from his father's more explosive petulance.

"Billy," I said, as gently as I could, not touching him so as not to startle him.

He wasn't as out of it as I thought, speaking like he knew I was there all along. "Is it true?" His voice, thick with emotion, caught a moment before he coughed into one fist and tried again, jamming that hand back into his jeans with force. "Is my dad…?"

I glanced at the diner door, noted the deputy watching, and waved for him to join me. He moved at once, heading in our direction, while I fished a card out of my wallet and offered it to Billy. When he looked down it took him a long time to accept it, but he did finally, just before the deputy came to a halt in front of us.

"Sheriff King can tell you everything," I said. "She'll find out who did this, Billy."

He shuddered, looked up at me, hazel eyes sad, so full of sorrow my heart broke for him. "Like they caught the person who killed my brother," he said in a voice so dead and empty I wished I'd said something different to comfort him. Though it was likely at this point nothing would except bringing in his father's killer. If someone killed Big Dan. For all I knew, the idiot broke into the diner to do damage to Ingrid's place in retaliation for Cherise kicking him out and got himself locked in the walk-in, tried to get out, lost his temper, had a heart attack or stroke and did this to himself.

Wouldn't help Billy any to know that was where my mind went. Or answer the question—where did Big Dan get keys or, without them, how did he get in since neither door was forced?

"If you need someone to talk to," I said, "please call, Billy. I'm happy to help."

He bobbed a brief nod, looking away, following the deputy to the front of the diner and inside, while I sighed out the empathy his tragic circumstance raised before getting in my SUV and heading home.

Calliope and Thalia were already there, Thalia's red Cooper Mini parked in the driveway, the pair in the living room snuggling Belladonna when I dumped my keys and wallet on the counter and crossed to join them. My daughter rose, hugged me, took the cat from her girlfriend, who also hugged me, the contrast between the stout, curly-haired child that I birthed to the tall, willowy blonde I hadn't but was just as much my kid as far as I was concerned inconsequential to me. What mattered was their happiness, their connection and as they sat again, sharing Belladonna between them, the white fluff flipped over so they could rub her chin and belly, I perched on the coffee table and waited for them to speak.

They exchanged a look, like they'd planned out what they were going to say and now didn't know how to start before the usual suspect spoke first.

"Dad saw us out to dinner two nights ago," Calliope blurted. Thalia's cheeks pinked, light blue gaze fixed on the cat who purred her comfort while my daughter fell silent, swallowing in a gulping manner that had my heart hurting.

"He may have seen us…" Thalia paused, glanced at Calliope.

"Kissing, Mom." My kid finally got it out. "He saw us kissing. Okay? We're a couple." She'd flushed herself, though Thalia's more delicate skin had that pristine glow to it, my daughter went blotchy red like I did down her throat and across her collarbone when distress triggered her. "We're in love, have been for a long time." Thalia finally looked up, their hands meeting over Belladonna, holding one another tight, waiting in growing tension for me to say something.

"Yes, dear," I said with a shrug. "I know. So, what's the problem again?"

CHAPTER NINE

Calliope gaped then laughed, a short and heavy sound that cut off when she sagged back into the sofa cushions. "I told you she already knew."

Thalia's secret little smile lit her blue eyes. "You don't mind?"

The very fact the two of them thought I would had me struggling for what to say. I finally sighed. "I love you," I said. "I'm not making light of what you told me. Coming out is a huge thing and I'm so proud of both of you for telling me and for accepting how you feel about one another. For supporting each other." They exchanged another look. "Why did you think you couldn't tell me?" Yeah, that came out a little sadly, I admit it, though I did my best to hide the bulk of my sorrow from them because this wasn't about me, not really.

While being about me. Yup.

Calliope instantly leaned forward, arms out, and hugged me tightly, Belladonna hastily repositioned into Thalia's lap so she wouldn't end up on the floor without warning, though somehow Thalia managed to hug me, too, while I juggled two lovely young women and a fluffy feline and my own emotional state.

Only cried a little.

"Oh, Mom," Calliope said, her voice thick in my ear. "I wanted to, I really did. It's not that we didn't trust you."

"We trust you with *everything*," Thalia whispered while my mind went to November and how she'd acquired her family's fortune while my daughter went on. Even as the young heiress inhaled, paused. Wait, was there more needing to be said?

My daughter didn't let her speak. "It's just…" Calliope sat back again, holding one of my hands in both of hers, Thalia cradling Belladonna who continued to purr. "There's still so much stigma around coming out." She bit her lower lip, eyes pleading with me to understand. "And we wanted to sort it out completely, make sure we'd made the right decision. That's why I wanted to live with Thalia at Vesterville House." She smiled at her girlfriend. "We were both worried if we moved in together, we might realize we weren't in love anymore." Thalia shook her head, reaching for Calliope's hand. "Okay, *I* was worried." Thalia laughed at that, and I did, too. "But Mom, we only love each other more."

"More every day," Thalia said.

Calliope relaxed somewhat then, but a lingering tension had her hesitating once again. There was more, I was sure of it.

"So, your father," I prompted. "Saw you kissing at dinner." What was he doing out? Not that it mattered to me, not really, but the sudden hope maybe he'd been on a date (praise the Lord and halleluiah) made an appearance when Thalia spoke this time.

"We didn't realize Trent was there," she said, long fingers sliding through Belladonna's fur, an act I knew from experience had an intensely soothing influence. "And we weren't overt about it." She blushed then, flashed a grin.

Calliope snorted. "We weren't making out or anything," she agreed. "But I know he saw us kiss, Mom because I caught him watching. But before I could approach him, he and the woman he was with left."

Woman. He was *with*. Whoop! My prayers were answered. And before you wonder if I was even the teensiest bit jealous, let me assure you, if he'd let me find him a girlfriend, I'd have done it and danced a jig of joy over the ashes of our marriage certificate.

Hey, I was happy single, okay? No judging.

I took another moment to gather my thoughts before speaking because the last thing I wanted to do was damage my daughter's relationship with her father. I might not have been married to him anymore, but she would always be his flesh-and-blood and for all I knew he had something else in mind.

"Your father loves you," I said, "both of you," squeezed Thalia's hand after freeing it from Belladonna's fur, "and he would never judge you for loving one another." I had to believe that. Because otherwise I really *didn't* know the man I'd used to share my life with and I wasn't sure I was fully prepared to accept that. While Trent was a lot of things, I wished he wasn't when we were together, a hateful homophobe wasn't one of them.

There was a huge difference between lack of emotional connection with someone who never understood you or your needs and choosing to judge your own daughter for who she loved.

"Maybe you're right," Calliope said, again with that anxiety. "Mom, I'm so sorry we didn't tell you."

"I just want you to be happy," I said. "You two have had a connection since the day you met. I'm so glad you found one another, and that love is the result." I leaned back, suddenly so tired I considered canceling my Friday session in favor of a nap, knowing I wouldn't be able to give my client the focus and attention she deserved.

"Are you okay?" Calliope reached for me again and I nodded, holding her hand and sagging. "I said I was sorry."

"It's not you, sweetie," I said. And filled the two of them in on what I'd found that morning.

They both gaped, wide-eyed and horrified, though I admit my kid was much more fascinated than her girlfriend, not unexpected.

When I finished, I thought of the young man at the counter, the wealthy kid Checks called Rider, and my question for Thalia from the night before popped out. "Did you recognize him?" I asked after making sure she knew who I meant.

Thalia nodded, nose wrinkling in visible distaste. "That's Rider Huntington," she said. "He's from Bangor." Like there was something wrong with being from Bangor. "His father's a real estate mogul, new money." Thalia clasped both hands over her mouth, giggling. "Sorry," she said, "I didn't mean to sound so…"

"One percent?" Calliope added an arch tone to her voice, faintly arrogant British accent layered over it so Thalia laughed again.

"That's what I get for being born a Vesterville," she said, shrugging her narrow shoulders under her thin white button-up. "A bit of snobbery comes with the territory."

"What else do you know about him?" I had no idea if it was even important, though Cherise's interest in Checks meant I could at least offer up something even if it had no connection to Big Dan's death.

"He's not someone I'd trust with a dead rat," Thalia said then, voice flattening out. "I have no idea why he'd be slumming in Wallace." Again the grimace. "But he has a big reputation for wild parties and getting into trouble his father's money gets him out of."

I didn't mention her uncle, Gaines Vesterville, had the same reputation, nor that it hid the truth about him quite nicely. Or, that her own family's fortune had apparently paved over some truly horrific things in the past that had only recently come to light.

None of that was necessary. Instead, with their confession done and many hugs and much love passed back and forth, I saw them out, Belladonna sitting at my feet while I held Calliope back one last moment.

"You're sure there's nothing else?" I wanted an out, to believe Trent wasn't this big of a jerk.

Calliope bit her lower lip, glancing out the door at Thalia behind the wheel. Then shook her head with a grim expression before hugging me and leaving, not another word spoken.

Heart heavy but needing to trust my daughter wasn't keeping something from me, that she'd told me everything and wasn't lying which meant her father really was a creep I was going to drop-kick into next week, I waved to the girls when they drove off.

Closed the door on the departing car and genial horn toot to stare down into my cat's bright green gaze while she slow blinked back.

As I struggled with a decision I knew I had to make but was finding harder than I thought it would be. To call or not to call and ream out the man I used to be married to so I wouldn't murder him in his office at the FBI? Or wait, get some rest and a handle on my temper before I had the whole story?

Because if I was right and didn't know my ex like I thought I did, Trent Garret daring to think I was on his side against our daughter and love? He had another thing coming.

CHAPTER TEN

I surprised myself by making it through my session for the day without the lack of focus I'd anticipated, saying a fond goodbye to Jenny Morris as she left, one of my most faithful clients who'd carried over to my holistic practice when I'd exited mainstream therapy for less traditional and, in my opinion, more effective methods.

The fact Jenny had finally healed her main source of PTSD trauma within one session of a new tool we'd used just last year, her remaining issues tackled once a month or on her terms when she felt she needed help more than enough evidence to me I was on the right track, not to mention the fact the majority of my clients—I was so happy to no longer refer to those I counseled as patients—had seen significant recovery thanks to the continuing evolution of my practice and exploration of new methods and tools I explored.

Which was the bulk of my Friday from the moment she left, sitting at my desk researching the latest techniques in holistic mental medicine, Belladonna curled up on the blanket I folded and laid out for her next to my computer so she could be near me, as always, refills on coffee my only reason for getting up until I finally sat back, 5PM come way too soon, from a fascinating article on a new subliminal technique that seemed to be gaining ground into rewiring the subconscious mind.

I really, really loved my job.

That meant there was just enough time to pop a roast in the oven while my favorite playlist had me dancing in the kitchen, gin and cranberry poured over ice for sipping joining me while I made a fool of myself spinning and singing at the top of my lungs, only my cat present to watch and judge. By the time I'd finished mashing the cauliflower and turnip mix I pretended was the perfect substitute for potatoes, salad chopped and waiting with dressing on the side (I was such a slave to the last fifteen pounds I'd love to lose) and set two spots at the peninsula, the doorbell rang.

With the music turned down so I wouldn't

deafen my guest, I ran to the hall and whipped open the door, saluting Cherise as she grinned back, hoisting a clear plastic container of salad that was her contribution for my approval.

Cherise ate my lacking in carbohydrates cooking without complaint, as always, our conversation steered purposely clear of work—both of ours—until the dishes were in the dishwasher and we'd had enough time to catch up on each other's non-professional news and gossip.

When she joined me in the living room, sinking into the oversized armchair with Belladonna perching next to her on the thickly stuffed armrest, she finally broached the topic *de jour*, our mutual agreement ended when food was consumed. "I heard back from Owen," she said. I took the couch, sitting cross-legged with a cushion to balance my drink on, nodding. Cherise's fingers slid through Belladonna's fur, not even my hard-core cop friend's soul immune to the lure of kitty comfort. While I knew she was more a dog person, her classically trained retired K-9 German Shepard and the old, toothless rescue chihuahua her daughter Layla adored their family's choice of pets, Cherise never failed to give Belladonna the attention she deserved when she visited. "Dan Abrams died of a heart attack." So not murder. That was a relief. "However." So much for the relief. "How he got into the walk-in in the first place I have no idea."

"Could the door have closed behind him on its own?" I didn't wait for her to answer. "And shouldn't there have been some kind of security feature that would let him get out if the door did somehow shut?"

She nodded over her drink, dark eyes thoughtful, one leg crossed, the foot bobbing up and down a little. "The latch inside was broken," she said. "Ingrid said it's been that way for a while, was meant to be fixed. Lots of meant tos in that place." Like the security cameras? I didn't comment, not wanting to judge my friend—either of them—as she went on. "I checked the door. There was no way it would swing shut without help. The spring that should have triggered it is snapped in half." Which answered the question definitively then, because it was highly unlikely Big Dan would have closed it on himself, right?

Someone else was there and that someone locked him in to die.

"Owen said he had significant damage to his hands and a broken toe inside his boot." Cherise sighed over her empty drink but shook her head when I rose to take it and refill it. She set it aside instead. "Thanks for dinner, but I can't stay. I have more work to do but I didn't want to cancel our usual Friday date."

"You're saying someone locked him in there alive," I said, ignoring her not-so-subtle exit request, "and he got so worked up trying to escape he had a heart attack."

She nodded.

"So not murder." Owen said if his heart held out, he'd likely still be alive, shouldn't he? With the way he was dressed and his body's composition, he'd have had frostbite, no doubt, and probably hypothermia, but he wouldn't have died. "Or are you thinking otherwise?"

Cherise pushed herself forward to the front of the chair, staring down into the ice in her glass. Belladonna sat up, bumping the sheriff with a soft head butt before hopping down to the floor and sashaying her way to me.

"I'm leaning toward an accident," she said, though she didn't sound convinced. "Let me ask you, though, Seph, if you purposely locked someone in a freezer, knowing they'd be there for the night without the insight and education someone like Owen had, would you expect them to be alive the next morning?"

I thought about it, then shook my head. "So attempted murder," I said.

She stood, carrying her glass to the kitchen.

"Let's call it manslaughter and leave it at that." She dumped the remaining ice into the sink with a rattle, doing the polite guest thing and setting it on the top rack of the dishwasher, her precision mind, I'd discovered early on, not allowing her to just leave in on the counter like I used to suggest. "Thanks, Seph," she said then. "I needed to talk that out."

"My pleasure." I walked her to the door, handed over her leather jacket. "Did Billy know anything?"

She shook her head as she settled her shoulders under the heavy coat, the hem falling to her ankles, making her look like some kind of sci-fi secret agent. If I didn't know her as well as I did, I might have been intimidated. "My working theory? Big Dan somehow got his hands on keys with the intent to make Ingrid's life miserable. He was in the walk-in with plans to do who knows what vandalism project he had in mind, and Ingrid caught him at it." Cherise's dark eyes held mine and I knew better than to protest. "She closed him in and left him there, probably out of fear."

"But, if that's the case," I said, "why would she open the next morning before getting rid of him?" There were holes in her logic that had me defensive despite myself. I did my best to be there for her, but honestly, the scenario she laid out had enough gaps in it I couldn't resist poking at them.

Cherise frowned, sighed, tossed her big hands. "I'm still looking into it," she said. "I'm not saying it's a perfect theory, Seph. That's why I'm heading back to the office. I have a few other people to look into."

"What about Saucy the cook?" Time to mention his reticence last night. "He took one look at you when you arrived at the opening and hot-footed it back into the kitchen like you were about to arrest him then and there."

Her head cocked, frown appearing. "You didn't tell me that."

"I didn't think it was important," I said. "But who knows what kind of background he has. Maybe Dan stumbled into something he wasn't supposed to find out about and got himself whacked." Okay, I'd clearly been watching too many police procedurals.

Cherise's grin told me she agreed, though she didn't say so out loud. "There's also Checks Johnson," she said. "He's just a kid, but he's had some misdemeanors and there are rumors he's trying to break into the drug trade." She didn't have to tell me how terrible that idea would be for him if he decided to follow through.

"Thalia knew the young man in the suit," I

said, speaking of drugs. "Rider Huntington? His father is a real estate developer in Bangor."

Cherise was nodding. "He's on my radar for other things," she said. "I have a suspicion he's been talking with Checks, but from what I can tell it's a different case altogether."

"Didn't Little Dan die in Bangor?" I know, I was reaching, but that was how my brain worked, making connections.

The sheriff's frown ended in a head shake. "Bangor's out of my jurisdiction, Seph. But yeah, too coincidental not to check all the bits and pieces I suppose." She laughed then, a sudden shift out of concentrated seriousness to playful teasing in a heartbeat. "You after my job, woman?"

I grinned myself, firmly denying it as I opened the door and gestured for her to get out, thank you. "Go catch some bad guys. I'm more than happy for you to play superhero while I watch from the sidelines."

"Could have fooled me," she said before leaving with a wave, the sound of her Charger's engine rumbling past the house as she drove off.

Well, she wasn't really wrong, though as I scooped up Belladonna who waited patiently for me to give her love now that her visitor was gone, I argued with myself that none of the cases I'd been involved in were intentional and that any participation I'd had in catching the killers had been either accidental or landed in my lap.

I was much more inclined to helping people heal than putting them behind bars, thanks.

Trouble was that Cherise's theory and my own agile mind had me tossing and turning and unable to sleep when I tried to go to bed early. It wasn't until about midnight I finally gave up and climbed out of the warm blankets, draping myself in my favorite silk robe, the pant legs of my matching pajama bottoms skimming the floor as I made my way downstairs and to my office.

Belladonna joined me, though she went right back to sleep on her blanket while I did my own digging into the Abrams family, reading about the death of first the mother to cancer when the boys were only little. Then the sister, Perry, who died of a tragic overdose at fourteen. Of Little Dan after perusing a few articles about his budding career as a baseball pitcher, an injury blowing out his elbow in his senior year of high school. The next mention of him came from the morning after the police found his body, article outlining his fall from possible major league potential to his untimely death on a side street. Someone had struck him in the back of the head and the blow, though bloodless, had knocked him to the ground. One last article a week later claimed the impact blew apart an aneurysm, according to the Bangor ME, he hadn't known he had that ended his life quickly.

As for Big Dan, there was little about him aside from the occasional ranting complaint that made it into the local paper, a photo of him and Billy at Little Dan's funeral, and a single mention of him in his youth and his football career that ended thanks to an injury that mirrored Little Dan's failure almost to a T.

The only one in the family who seemed to have landed on his feet was Billy, the whole reason for my deep dive into his kin. If he did call, at least I'd be prepared somewhat. Trouble was, I'd barely had a chance to put his name into the search engine when my doorbell rang.

At one in the morning.

Had me running for the door, panic making my stomach churn, mind flashing to worst-case scenarios about Calliope and car accidents or some other tragedy that might have someone come to my house in the middle of the night.

When I whipped the door open, I realized my mistake and that desperate anxiety I felt switched from terror for my daughter to personal fear. Because the very last person I expected stood on the other side of the door, Saucy's tense and threatening presence such a shock I squeaked.

While he flashed something at me from under his coat, the badge shiny enough to catch light and make me gape in surprise.

"Ms. Pringle," he said, soft and intense, the lowbrow accent and slurring language he'd used in the diner missing from his speech, "my name is Detective Joseph Atlas with Maine state police. I know it's late, but I really need to talk to you."

CHAPTER ELEVEN

The last thing I expected in the wee hours of the morning was to be serving coffee to an undercover state detective while he rubbed my cat's belly to her deafening purrs and sat down to hear why it was he couldn't out himself to Cherise.

"I realize she's trustworthy," he said, his tattooed and muscular look augmented with a beat-up leather jacket he retained despite my offer to hang it at the door, grubby jeans and boots under a faded button-up and white t-shirt giving him the rough look of someone on the other side of the law than his badge suggested. But his shift in speech from street-thug to educated and rather cultured had me enamored of the dichotomy his outside presented compared to this rather articulate communication, his tenor voice intense but controlled. "It's not that I don't think your sheriff can keep my secret. But the more she looks into me, the harder it's going to be to maintain my cover and I really need her to back off."

"Can't you have one of your superiors at state tell her what's going on?" I knew better than to be drinking coffee this late, but I was already tired and if I didn't have something to pick me up, I'd be incoherent. "I'm not a police officer or member of the sheriff's department, detective."

"Maybe not," he said, "but I know your reputation and that Sheriff King often asks you to read in when she has need of an expert to talk to suspects." He'd been looking into me, had he? "You've been involved in enough murder cases I'm confident in your ability, Ms. Pringle."

"Persephone," I said. "Pringle. And your confidence, while kindly flattering, might be misplaced. I'm not sure how you expect me to have her back off if I can't tell her who you really are." I might have been a therapist and Cherise's friend, but I wasn't a miracle worker. The sheriff had a penchant for digging despite evidence to the contrary that I might only inspire if I didn't tell her everything.

"Joe." He saluted me with his coffee. "I just need her off my back for another twenty-four hours or so. If you can distract her with something?" He sighed then, shook his head, setting aside his mug. "Look, I knew this was a long shot. You have no reason to trust me. But it's important." Joe gave Belladonna another scritch under her chin to her delight, green eyes heavy, purr unrelenting as she did a soft air-knead with both front paws. "I've met Sheriff King a few times, so I know she'll recognize me. And start asking questions I can't answer."

That didn't sound promising, especially if he really was here officially. Then again, undercover work meant a lot of secrets, didn't it? "Can I ask a few?" He shrugged so I went on, taking that as the affirmative. "Why would state police send you here if you're familiar with local law enforcement? They must have realized you'd run into this exact scenario."

His hesitation had my instincts buzzing. "It's a long story," he said.

I set my mug down, the firm thud of it making Belladonna jump and Joe look up with a closed and guarded expression. "You're not being completely honest with me," I said, "and while I appreciate your effort, I hope you don't think I'm an idiot." He flinched a little. "If you came here thinking you could just waltz out a story about being undercover and have me on side without a full explanation, you have another thing coming. Joe." I didn't mean to let my temper get the better of me, but it seemed to work because he relented somewhat, sighing, rubbing both hands over his face, visibly weary when he dropped them to his lap, dark eyes smiling though wryly instead of with humor.

"Like I said, a long shot." He took another sip of coffee. "There's only so much I can tell you."

"Only so much you choose to tell me," I said. "What are you investigating?"

Another pause, but he answered at least. "A drug ring."

"In Wallace?" I actually snorted, finding the idea ridiculous in a flash of denial, while his steady and confident gaze convinced me otherwise.

"I get it," he said, sounding a little sad. "It's a familiar reaction, believe me. Most small towns like yours, folks don't want to believe it. But distributing through places like this happens all the time. It's the perfect cover because no one would ever imagine such a thing happening in their community. Right?"

I nodded slowly, horror growing inside me. "That's... terrible."

"And far more common than you think," he said. "Goes on in small towns all around the country. This one in particular is run by a guy out of Bangor and he's the one I'm really after."

Not hard to put the pieces together. "Rider Huntington," I said.

Joe arched an eyebrow at me before laughing. "Very clever. Your reputation isn't nearly as solid as it should be."

My turn to shrug. "Maybe that's a good thing."

Joe's wink and grin told me he agreed. "Huntington's slick," he said, "knows how to hide his tracks. I've got nothing on him, just a weak trail and a whole lot of anecdotal evidence I can't use in court. He's got this new drug, calls it CakePop. Gives a physical high like ecstasy but as dangerous as fentanyl at higher doses." I wasn't up on drug culture, though I had, of course, treated clients suffering from addiction so the names were familiar enough. "I've been tracing the delivery routes and I know I'm close."

"Is Checks Johnson involved?" Cherise mentioned his desire to be the local gangster despite the fact this was Wallace, so come on, gangster? Joe, however, took the question seriously, bobbing a nod.

"I'm looking into that," he said. "I just need a little more time. There are... circumstances surrounding this case that mean if I report in before I have what I need I may be pulled from the field and the entire operation lost."

That sounded sketchy to me. Not just because if his bosses were planning to pull him out of the case, what was he doing that would trigger such a move? I couldn't help but wonder if Joe was dirty, though if he was on the take, why come to me at all? Regardless, I barely knew him, and I adored Cherise. And no amount of convincing would have me agree to lying to her. He'd overestimated his play if he thought I would just jump on board. Nope, not even for a state detective. Heck, not for any reason.

Sure, because I hadn't lied to her in November. Okay, withholding the truth wasn't exactly lying, but it was close enough I knew better than to hold myself to the high standard I tried to defend.

Only made me more determined, because *guilt*. He must have seen my rejection in my face because he sat back, crossing his arms over his chest, Belladonna chirping her dissatisfaction with his lack of attention.

"I can't lie to her," I said. "But if you'll let me tell her who you are, I'll convince her to give you that twenty-four hours." He thought about it a moment, then sighed, nodded. "Do you think Dan Abrams had anything to do with your case?"

Joe had clearly been wondering the same thing. "I don't think so," he said. "As far as I could tell, dude just had a big mouth. I've been on this case for six months, and I know I'm close. The death was just a stupid coincidence, but one that could mean Huntington gets away with what he's up to. I can't live with that."

"Fine," I said, buying his earnestness as long as I could do what he asked my way. "I'll talk to her. But I suggest you work fast because Cherise isn't going to hold off for long if something about Big Dan's death ties into what you're doing."

Joe stood, offered his hand and I shook it before he dropped one of his cards on the counter. "If I can't find everything I need by tomorrow night, I'll go see her personally. Fair?"

I escorted him to the door, closing it firmly behind him as he hurried off, debating texting her immediately and trading that choice for an early-morning visit.

While wondering how I'd gotten myself wrapped up in yet another mess without even trying.

CHAPTER TWELVE

I did make one call the next morning before leaving to see Cherise, the nice young woman on reception at Maine State Police confirming a Detective Joseph Atlas did, in fact, work for the department.

"I'm afraid he's not available right now," she said in her cheery voice after a moment of silence. "Leave of absence. Can I take a message for him?"

"No, thank you," I said. "I'll call back." And hung up, satisfied that much about his story was true, even as I did a quick internet search of the roster and found a picture of him as a young uniform, my paranoia making me uncomfortable. When had I grown to be so suspicious? Maybe the four dead bodies I'd now stumbled over had something to do with it.

Cherise was in interrogation when I landed at the station, just exiting with young Checks Johnson following her, the sheriff watching him go as he slumped his way out. He glanced at me, hands stuffed into the front pocket of his hoody, sullen expression barely hiding the anxiety behind his eyes. Some hard-core criminal. The kid was terrified and barely able to disguise it with that street-smart punk act of his.

Which had me wondering about his involvement with Rider Huntington and if Joe Atlas was wrong about the kid. I'd heard them arguing over territory. The likelihood Checks was working with Rider seemed slim to me after overhearing that conversation. But that didn't mean Checks didn't have something to do with Big Dan ending up in the walk-in.

Cherise brightened at the sight of me, waving me in to sit across from her at her desk, closing the door behind her as I offered up a large coffee. Her grin of greeting faded quickly when I sat back with a grim expression and told her about my visitor.

To her credit, she listened all the way through before commenting, though the low thrum of anger in her deep alto was Cherise King at her least happy.

"He might be right about Checks," she said. "Cameras at the post office across the street from the diner have him entering the alley that night around midnight, but he wasn't the only one." She tapped the surface of a file with one fingertip hard enough it made the paper slide forward. "Gabriella Torres was also on the footage, though she was there closer to 11PM around the time Ingrid was seen leaving. But your detective friend? He was there at midnight, just like Checks." Oh, and she was delighted by that fact, let me tell you, black eyes narrowed and snapping anger, her dark cheeks flushed, full lips in a thin and dangerous line.

"What about Big Dan?" How had he gotten in?

Cherise shook her head in a short, angry motion, her chair creaking just a little in protest. "No sign of him," she said. "He must have entered from the other end of the alley. No cameras there."

"Which means whoever killed him could have used that way as well," I said.

She didn't comment, didn't have to. Despite the footage, her job wasn't getting any easier and I just dumped a further complication in her lap.

"And Billy has no idea why his father was there?" It had to be a retaliation effort for getting kicked out. That was exactly something Big Dan would do.

Cherise didn't answer that unanswerable question. Instead, she sat forward, reaching for her phone, standing and pacing across the room, voice low when she made a call while I sat and sipped my coffee and did my best not to interfere.

Five minutes later, she took her seat, setting aside her cell and frowning at it like it offended her somehow. "That was… frustrating." She met my eyes, her own thoughtful. "According to the detective I spoke to, Atlas is supposed to be in Bangor."

He'd suggested that, hadn't he? Sort of. "You're thinking he's rogue or something?"

"Or something," she said, grim and heavy. Ah. Dirty, my same worry. She sat back once more, rocking into her chair until the creaking turned to a hearty groaning from the rotating base. "So, what's he doing in Wallace?"

"Huntington is here," I suggested. "Maybe the twenty-four-hour window has something to do with his presence."

She grunted, took a long drink of her coffee. "Seph," she said. "I'm not mad. You did the right thing. But this whole situation troubles me. Like, a lot. Someone undercover running off on his own agenda… it looks bad.

And I'm worried because he dragged you into it when he shouldn't have involved a civilian."

"You think he's on the take," I came out and said it. "The same thought crossed my mind, Cherise."

Her giant exhale had her relaxing somewhat, but her tight smile told me otherwise. "His original gig is legit, at least. So, it could be he's chasing something tied to it and didn't want to tell his bosses because it would mean compromising his case. I get that. But the fact he didn't go through channels… it wouldn't be the first time someone undercover switched teams for money or power. So let me ask you." Those dark eyes fixed me with a seriousness that had me holding my breath. "What do you think I should do?"

Wait, she was asking me? "You want to know if I trust him or not?"

She spread her hands wide before grasping her cup firmly, as if trying to keep them still. "I trust your judgment," she said. "If you think I should give him twenty-four, I'll do it. But that's my limit."

"I told him you'd say that," I said. Thought about it a long moment. Sure, Cherise trusted me, of course, she did, and the feeling was mutual. But this was the first time she was laying it out for me in a professional capacity.

Talking with witnesses in her presence was one thing. Taking my opinion to heart when it came to a possible suspect, quite another. Did I believe Joe Atlas had other intentions other than resolving his case?

I made a decision, uncrossing my legs and sitting up straighter. "If he hasn't come to talk to you by midnight, call him in to his handler."

Cherise nodded once, sat up herself. "Done," she said. Didn't add, *I hope we don't regret this*. Didn't have to.

I'd already said that to myself.

With nothing else to offer, I left, heading to Trent's office because I might as well add insult to injury and deal with both weighty situations in one morning. His resident agency had only a handful of agents, the fact he retained an office there despite his ranking in the organization tied to the agreement we'd made when Calliope was born. Choosing to travel instead of move, I knew Trent gave up opportunities over the years to advance his career. Despite his continuing choice to live in Wallace, and maybe because of it, he'd instead fallen into his particular specialty, leading a small team who investigated major crimes around New England.

Which meant, despite the fact I knew he was in the office every day he was in Wallace (yes, even Saturdays), when I arrived to have our little chat, the young man who had been left behind to man the desk informed me Trent and the rest of the team were out of state until tomorrow.

"Thanks, Jimmy," I said, heading out, frustrated and disappointed since I'd worked myself up to having this conversation with my ex, wishing it was over with now and not lingering in an anxious puddle in the back of my mind, sloshing around and causing moments of intense unrest when I forgot it was there. The sight of a wanted poster on the wall had me pause, six faces filling the spaces but only one causing me to inhale a little in surprise.

It could easily have been a case of mistaken identity, but the longer I stared at Carlita Sanchez, the more certain I was I'd seen her before. Comforted her, in fact, when Big Dan yelled at her, hugged her in the kitchen at The Blueberry Grill. And now needed to call Cherise again, because if I was right? Gabriella Torres had been lying about her identity, too. Only she was no undercover detective but wanted for a selection of offenses, not the least of which was fraud.

But when I whipped out my phone, taking a quick photo to share with Cherise, it rang, surprising me enough I jumped. Answered with a catch in my voice, still staring at Carlita and now wondering if she was somehow tied to Big Dan or maybe even Rider Huntington and wasn't Cherise going to love hearing from me again…?

"Ms. Pringle," the caller said, the young man's voice sounding familiar, but it took me a moment, still distracted, before I realized who was calling, just before he said his name. "It's Billy Abrams. I was wondering… I'd like to take you up on your offer if you don't mind."

"Of course, Billy," I said.

"Are you free now? I know it's Saturday and everything." The sound of a car door slamming and the engine firing up told me he was on the move. "I really need someone to talk to."

"Meet me at my home office," I said, decision made. Gave him the address. "A half-hour?"

"Thank you." He hung up while I finished my text to Cherise and headed home, adding this new bit of info as an afterthought. Whether it mattered to her or not, I wasn't keeping anything from the sheriff where this case was involved, at least within the realm of what I was allowed to tell her.

Now, as long as Billy didn't tell me in session something it would be illegal and unethical to share but could solve the murder… why was it dread seemed to be the most common emotion I carried around these days?

CHAPTER THIRTEEN

Billy was waiting in my driveway when I got home, standing outside his car, leaning against the door, chewing his fingernails and visibly agitated as I parked my SUV next to him. From the moment I greeted him, shaking his hand, he didn't meet my eyes, his own hazel ones downcast, looking around like some threat loomed, even after I escorted him through the side door and into my private office space, cut off from the rest of the house by a doorway to maintain some distance from my personal life.

Belladonna instantly scratched to be let in which I allowed, though I carefully observed Billy as he took a seat on the edge of the sofa I supplied for clients, hands clasped, elbows on his knees which bounced up and down violently enough even my cat kept her distance.

When she chose to perch on my chair and observe him instead of leaping up beside him, her green eyes slits of watchful feline judgment, I took her reticence to offer him comfort as her way of saying he was beyond even her powers to calm or soothe.

It wasn't often Belladonna avoided a client, but I hardly blamed her, especially when I'd barely taken a seat next to her when he surged to his feet and began to pace.

"The sheriff is talking to Checks Johnson," Billy blurted. "Does he think he killed my father?" He didn't wait for me to answer, spinning and crossing the room in a couple of strides before stopping and hugging himself. "She won't tell me anything. I just want to know what happened." His pacing fired up again, face red, voice stuttering and cracking with barely contained emotion. The faint scent of body odor wafted from him, his messy hair and the clothes he wore bearing the marks of someone who hadn't taken care of themselves, wrinkled and stained sweatshirt under his denim jacket, bedhead all indicators he'd likely not slept and even more so not showered since his father's death telling me he probably hadn't eaten either.

"Billy," I said. Started to say, searching for the right inroad, but was cut off when he spun on me, anger flashing over his young face.

"I saw you go into the sheriff's office," he said, nearly an accusation, definitely aggressive. "What did she tell you? She must have told you something."

Rarely did I feel uncomfortable with clients. Only on occasions of extreme stress or grief had I ever been in a position where the person I counseled made me feel unsafe. This was one of those moments, Billy's simmering agitation rising to the surface as a level of rage I could see growing on him like a gaping tumor.

"You're not here to talk," I said, standing, Belladonna hopping down and scooting to a corner where she wrapped her tail around her paws and glared while I did my best to keep calm, hands spread out in front of me even as I slowly circled toward the office door. That one, at least, I'd left open, an easy exit to the outside just a hallway away, or the main house through the other door lockable and hopefully protection enough if he did become violent. "Perhaps you should go."

Billy blinked when I started moving, retreating himself, sitting suddenly. "I'm sorry," he said, voice trembling. "I didn't mean to scare you." He sobbed then, into both hands, shaking. "I just need to know what's going on." Billy looked up, grief tearing at him, face contorted with it, my empathy surging back into place though I was smart enough to not allow it to smother my sense of self-preservation. Instead of joining him as I would another client, I handed him a box of tissues and sat again, waiting for him to compose himself, blowing his nose and staring down at the box in his lap while he shook and took a few trembling breaths that hitched more than once.

"Billy," I tried again. This time he didn't interrupt, nodded a little. "Sheriff King is doing everything she can to find out what happened to your father. I promise you, she's on your side."

He grunted something, jaw setting, shallow breaths coming in short pants. "Like the cops in Bangor gave a crap about what happened to Little Dan." He looked away, Adam's apple bobbing violently when he swallowed with convulsive effort. "No one gives a crap what happened to him, either, and don't tell me they care what happened to my dad."

I exhaled softly, wishing there were words of comfort I could offer, but frankly, his father wasn't well-liked. Not that it would influence Cherise in any way but offering a platitude about Big Dan would ring hollow and the last thing I wanted was to upset Billy further.

Instead, I tried another tactic. "Checks was at the diner," I said, silently winging off a wince and a whispered plea for forgiveness to Cherise for sharing information with the victim's son. Billy seemed to latch onto that, his dark and terrible hurt retreating somewhat.

"Did he... does she think he killed Dad?" No hope there, not really. Just dread, and a deep-seated sense of what felt like self-hate. The poor kid. He'd lost his whole family to tragedy and couldn't even bring himself to believe someone might pay for his losses.

"She doesn't know yet," I said. "Do you know Checks at all, Billy?"

He shrugged, hands clasping the box of tissues so tightly it crumpled a little. I jumped slightly when Belladonna crept forward and tucked herself between my feet, leaning into me, still watching him from her crouch. Billy didn't seem to notice her return, coughing softly to clear his throat before speaking.

"Kind of, not really." He set the damaged tissue box aside, clasping his hands in his lap as he sat stiffly back, knees jumping again. "He worked for me for a bit, but I had to let him go. Not reliable."

"Worked for you?" Hmmm. Doing what, I wondered.

"I have a small reno company," Billy said.

"Checks was helping me when I subcontracted at the diner. He lasted like two days." Billy stared at the floor, and it was only then I realized the kid was likely in shock and had been for far too long than was healthy for him.

All while drawing a straight line from Checks Johnson to The Blueberry Grill's walk-in and another young man who popped into my head.

CHAPTER FOURTEEN

"What about Rider Huntington?" Billy flinched at the name, but answered again, this time with dull fury coloring his words.

"I've seen him around," he said. Sniffled, wiped at his nose with a fresh tissue. "I've been dating Gabriella, and he gave her a hard time. Guy's a jackass." Tell me how you really feel about him, Billy. I couldn't help the renewal of compassion I felt. Animosity and distrust had become his daily staple, and I wondered if he'd make it out of the darkness he'd fallen into without real help. Likely not, though if he wasn't going to actually commit to the session, there was nothing I could do.

He surged to his feet then, as if he'd decided the same thing, tossing the used tissues into the waste basket beside the sofa, bobbing a fast nod, head still down, shoulders tense, hands jammed into the pockets of his jeans under the hem of his dark blue sweatshirt. "Sorry I bothered you," he said. "This was a bad idea." Billy spun and left, leaving me a little breathless when the thudding sound of the exterior door closing told me he'd departed. Though, I held still aside from scooping my cat into my lap and snuggling her until the sound of his truck engine driving away went quiet.

"Tough one, huh, Bella?" I let her down, the cat shaking herself all over before exiting my office for the main house. I followed her, realizing my own hands trembled, and that I needed to sit again by the time I reached the kitchen peninsula. Not that I really believed Billy would have hurt me, but the intensity of his emotions and the barely controlled outpouring of his aggravated state left me with enough adrenaline in my system I had to take a few deep breaths before calling Cherise.

Had to leave a voicemail, filling her in on his visit but not the contents, only that he'd been asking questions before hanging up. And thought about my research into the death of Little Dan Abrams. Blunt force trauma, a single blow, one the police believed was either delivered by someone who snuck up behind him or a person he trusted.

No other clues, no suspects, nothing. Just a dead young man and now a deceased father, both unusual deaths that seemed to have no rhyme or reason. And had me wondering all over again if the losses of both Dans were connected.

Though I had the rest of the day to myself, the idea of staying home had me restless, the encounter with Billy and my own lingering doubts about Joe Atlas and my involvement in the case driving me out of the house and onto the road, if only to distract myself from the low-level anxiety that seemed to pair with the dread I did my best to ease but failed miserably to resolve.

Checking in on Ingrid seemed a logical step. When I stopped at her house, I noted her car was missing and no one answered the door. That had me parking in front of the diner next to her dark blue sedan, the next logical stop the right one, apparently, my friend as unable to stay away from her new business as I'm certain I would have been too under those same circumstances. I circled to the alleyway when the front door remained locked, no sign of deputies any longer, the door to the kitchen giving way when I gingerly tested the knob.

"Ingrid?" I stepped in, the dim interior engulfing me, a dramatic shift from the bright morning outside, forcing me to blink to adjust. Why she hadn't turned any lights on I didn't know, the windowless back area of the diner making it hard to maneuver until my eyes adjusted with only the illumination through the round glass in the kitchen door letting in the late morning sun. Maybe she was out front? I'd been back here enough times that I was able to move ahead even before I could see fully, only stopping in my tracks at the sight of Ingrid.

Standing on a ladder. Under an open ceiling panel. Panic on her face.

"Ingrid?" I spoke again, softly so as not to startle her too much, hearing her squeak of surprise regardless, how she twitched before grabbing at the top of the stepladder in a forced crouch, huge hazel eyes staring into mine with the same level of fear she'd shown the other night when she'd emerged from the walk-in hours before the discovery of Big Dan.

"Seph." The whole ladder trembled as she clung to it, but she didn't come down. "What are you doing here?"

I approached slowly, the vibration in her voice, the panic on her face, how her gaze darted around as if terrified someone else might show up. And find what?

"I wanted to check on you," I said, coming to a halt under the ladder, reaching up to support her. She shook her head, tears leaking down her cheeks now, desperate horror on her face. "Ingrid, whatever happened, whatever's going on, you can trust me. I only want to help."

"I can't… you don't…" she licked her lips. Looked up. Drawing my gaze to the open ceiling panel. Was that something on the beam above? Something bulky and black? "You can't be here. Seph, you have to go." She grabbed hastily for the ceiling above her, rocking the ladder, dragging the panel she'd shoved beneath the next one over to mostly cover the gap. "The light," she blurted. "It's not working properly."

I didn't bother reminding her the panel she handled didn't have a light and neither was there one anywhere near where she stood. Instead, I offered my hand, guided her down as she stumbled and almost fell, jerking away from me when she reached the floor.

"Cherise still won't let me open," she said, voice a near-wail of despair. "Seph, I'm in so much debt and I don't know what to do." She flinched as though some thought she couldn't bear crossed her mind. Yes, it could have been panic about her financial situation that had her so worked up, but I had a feeling it was so much more than that.

"Ingrid." I let her have a moment to focus on me, on the sound of my voice. "Ingrid, were you here when Big Dan broke in?"

She gaped at me, sobbed, shook her head. "I had nothing to do with it," she said, voice cracking. "*Nothing.*" Ingrid went rigid, wiping at tears with the shoulder of her t-shirt. "I can't believe you asked me that. We've known each other forever. I can't believe you think I'd… I'd…"

I tried to grasp for her hand, to comfort her, but she backpedaled until she ran into the sink, pressing herself into it, arms tight around her narrow torso, breathing coming in short gasps. Reminding me of Billy in so many ways I backed off.

"I don't believe it," I said as firmly as possible, facing her down, forcing her to listen as I closed the distance between us and blocked her from running away. I might have been afraid of Billy, but there was nothing about Ingrid that made me worry for my safety.

No, I was worried about hers.

She moaned then, arms falling away from that tight squeeze and hands rising to cover her face. "Why is this happening to me?" She let me hug her and I did, Ingrid's desperate grip turning into tension as she finally pushed me back but grasped my shoulders in her hands a moment, face resolute, jaw set. "I didn't do anything wrong, Seph. But I think I might have gotten Big Dan killed." And then she sobbed again and didn't stop for a long time.

When she finally collected herself, I had her seated on the kitchen's only stool, rubbing her back and murmuring comforting words to her, instructing her to breathe while she went through a seemingly endless pile of tissues I replaced over and over again while Ingrid's stressed and terrified weeping ran its course. I let her reach the hiccupping release stage before I asked the obvious question as gently as possible.

"Why is it you think Big Dan's death was your fault?"

She stared at me, a little blank now, but no longer hysterical before she lurched to her feet and returned to the ladder. Climbed it on shaking knees while I almost told her to come back down, worried she might fall but curious, now, burningly so, about what it was she'd been doing up there. Waited while she pushed the panel back, reached up.

And pulled down a rather hefty black duffle bag that had her grunting and using both hands while I held her legs to support its weight.

She climbed down, set the bag on the floor between us. Nudged it with her sneaker, that horrified look returning mixed with awe and shock.

I crouched, unzipped it, drew a sharp breath in surprise while she spoke.

"I found that in the walk-in Thursday night," she said as I tugged open the top and examined the bundles of cash, the bags filled with tiny portions of some pink and yellow pills and, cringing from the touch of it, a handgun nestled into the middle of the stash. "I panicked." She caught her breath again, fresh tears trickling but her sobs resolved. "I didn't know what to do. I knew if I told Cherise she would investigate and close the diner and I was already in so much debt." Ingrid moaned again, sinking to the floor next to the bag. "So, I hid it in the ceiling, thinking I'd get rid of it the next day." She held out both hands and wrung them. "Yes, yes, I admit it," she blurted as if I'd accused her when it was her own internal accusation that had her carrying on. "I thought about keeping it. About getting rid of the drugs and the gun and using the money. It would make such a big difference." Ingrid seemed to find a bit of peace saying that out loud. "But I couldn't, Seph. I just couldn't." I nodded, happy to hear that as tempting as the opportunity had been. Who wouldn't have let the thought linger? "It was stupid, Seph, doing what I did. Stupid! Whoever put it in the walk-in must have come looking for it."

"You think Big Dan put it there?" I found it hard to comprehend he might be a drug dealer, but then again until I talked to Joe Atlas early this morning, I had no idea there was a ring of manufacturing and distribution right here in Wallace, so my surprise didn't mean much.

"I don't know," she said. "I doubt it. I don't know how he'd get access to my walk-in."

Not him, maybe, but someone with keys. Someone who had a connection to drug dealing and who worked with a construction company and could have easily made a copy of the key to the back door. Someone like Checks Johnson.

"What if whoever put it there came looking and Big Dan paid for my mistake?" Ingrid's shaking had her almost impossible to understand, constant hitch in her voice forcing me to focus on her alone and not my own thoughts to make out what she said. "What if my meddling got him killed?"

I hugged her again. "What if *his* meddling got him killed, you mean?" I let that sink in a moment. "Ingrid, you didn't do anything wrong." Well, she hadn't called Cherise right away, but I needed my friend calm, not thinking I blamed her for anything. "If Big Dan broke in here and ran afoul of whoever it was who hid this in your walk-in, that's on him. Right?" It took her a moment, but she finally nodded. "You didn't kill him or have anything to do with his death. The idiot shouldn't have been here in the first place." Another nod. Good, I was getting through to her. "Ingrid, we need to call Cherise."

Her initial rebellion to the idea faded quickly and, resigned, she finally sniffled one last time, reaching for her pocket and her phone.

"Sheriff King, please," she whispered into it when someone answered on the other end. "I have information about the death of Big Dan Abrams."

And so much more.

Except, it wasn't Cherise who walked into the kitchen a moment later. Instead, with a giant exhale of air that sounded far too much like relief, Detective Joe Atlas crossed to us in a hurry, crouching next to the bag, his dark eyes meeting mine with a giant grin.

"Finally," he said. "You just saved my job."

CHAPTER FIFTEEN

Cherise stood quietly and listened—one of her superpowers, I swear—while first Ingrid told her about finding the bag the night of the party and panic-hiding it in the ceiling before Joe unfolded the rest of his story to all three of us.

"My undercover op in Bangor didn't go according to plan," he said like that was a surprise considering the possessive way he stared at the bag now placed firmly beside the glowering sheriff. "I made a big bust, all on my own. Finally thought I had cracked their distribution cycle." He tossed both hands, meeting first the sheriff's eyes, then mine, while Ingrid perched on her stool again and rocked a little, watching and listening but not speaking and I wasn't even sure if she heard us in the state she'd fallen into. "Only to discover someone managed to steal a bag of evidence—the evidence I'd taken and was planning to turn in." He gestured at the bag. "That evidence."

"How are you so sure it's the same one?" I asked that question while Cherise continued her silent treatment.

Joe bent, looking up at her for permission. The sheriff nodded once while he tipped over one of the handles, shining a black light from his keychain on the woven polyester. JA reflected back in block letters. "I marked it just in case," he said. Sighed heavily, stood, tucking his keys away again. "I'm not kidding, Seph. You saved my butt. I don't know how to thank you."

"Thank Ingrid," I said. "After telling us how it ended up in Wallace—and how you knew to follow it here."

Cherise grunted ever so faintly, though she wasn't glaring at me, and when she didn't speak or move, I could only imagine she was barely holding back from demanding answers I asked rather nicely for.

In comparison, that was. I didn't exactly ask, after all, my own voice harsh with anger because this was ridiculous. But if it had been Cherise speaking, I was sure he'd be in far more serious trouble, so yeah. Call me nice.

Joe hesitated, then relented, visibly all in. "Little Dan Abrams," he said. "The kid worked in the network transporting drugs and cash when a bag he was transporting went missing. The same night someone killed him."

Well, that was kind of important for us to know. "Something you decided to keep from us," I said. He wasn't really endearing himself further, only digging himself a deeper hole.

"I took a leap and came to Wallace, thinking I might be able to connect one of the locals to the disappearance." He paused, swallowed at the sight of Cherise's furious face. "Since this wasn't the first time that evidence tied to the network went missing nor the first time Checks Johnson's name popped up in connection."

If I thought my sheriff friend was angry before, I hadn't seen anything yet. She swayed, like a tall tree in a stiff wind, as though the roots she'd planted through the soles of her boots prepared to tear free of the ground and send her crashing with violent assault on the smaller and reluctant detective.

"I need that evidence," he said to her, clearly missing the warning signs that were Hurricane Cherise barreling toward him with that same implacable determination as a category five ready to pulverize anything in her way. "I can't go back without it. I wasn't supposed to act on the intel I received, was meant to wait for backup. I took a risk and it paid off. Until it didn't." Oh, that was a terrible, terrible thing to admit to someone like Cherise King, let me tell you, her freight train of roaring inevitability heading for the ultimate crash and burn that was her imminent explosion. Not to mention the last bit of pause that had him squaring his shoulders, mouth drawn down in a scowl of his own. "I know how this looks," he said. "I also know you called my handler. Which means very shortly you're going to get a call telling you I'm dirty and I took off with the merch. But I didn't, I swear it." He looked back and forth between us. "I'm here to take it back to Bangor and clear my name."

There was the tornado of spinning rage that could toss Joe like debris about as easily as crush him to smithereens in 1.5 seconds.

Yes, I was aware the metaphors I used all tied into nature and/or large things that did a lot of damage because that was exactly how I pictured Joe Atlas meeting his end. Under the crushing and unstoppable force that was the sheriff of Wallace, Maine.

"You can't believe Cherise is going to let you take any of that," I spluttered. "Especially considering what you just told us." Sure, he might have been telling the truth, but he could also be covering his butt and assuming we'd buy it. Not. "If you're right about Little Dan, there's every chance at this point his death and his father's are connected. To that." I jabbed an index finger at the bag while Ingrid groaned in sympathetic counterpoint. "And since you can't prove to us you didn't steal it, how about you finish the rest of the story before Cherise throws you in jail."

Figured she'd do just that. Waited for the inevitable.

"It is courtesy," the sheriff said instead of cuffing him, quiet but deadly, surprising me when she spoke, "to contact local law enforcement when you're working a case in another jurisdiction, Detective Atlas." Every word clipped off in crisp perfection, my friend's steady flow of words cut clean at each edge, so sharp they cut the air between her and Joe Atlas in precise syllables that had me wincing. "Just as it should be apparent to you, detective, that this evidence is no longer yours to hand in but mine to deal with," she almost spit those two words, fury getting the better of her until she visibly wrangled it under the gigantic pressure of her command, "while working without the complete content of information I need," another jagged show of temper beyond her vibrating rigidity, "to solve a murder. Maybe two murders. While you've been *withholding*," yikes, she was going to blow any second now, Mt. Cherise a bubbling pit of magma waiting to explode, "vital clues that could help solve two deaths not to mention end a possible illegal drug manufacture and distribution ring in my town." The last two words ended in finger jabs at the ground before she clamped her arms tight across her chest again, swaying just a little. I watched her breathe, nostrils flaring, before she went on, voice even lower, more menacing, the caldera of her rage sinking below the surface again. Not necessarily a good thing, but at least this conversation wouldn't end in murder. "You were out of line on so many levels, not just with me. Now, if you have any more details to share, Detective Atlas, I suggest you give them up now before I call your superiors and have your butt fired and then arrested for so many misconducts I can't *even*."

While I was sure he'd been dressed down before—someone like him probably had it coming on a regular basis—the way he licked his lips and took a second before he spoke, hands on his hips but expression tense and anxious, he had to be feeling the full brunt of Cherise's displeasure and believed her. Smart boy.

"I've only been on this case six months," he said. "I wasn't around when Dan Abrams died." Little Dan, that was. "I swear, I didn't purposely keep anything from you. I didn't think his death was connected in any way to his father's loss." He glanced at me as if looking for backup, but he could look elsewhere, thanks. "I'm not here about some blowhard getting caught in a walk-in freezer and his ticker shutting down. I'm here about that." He jabbed at the bag.

"That," I said, "was found in said walk-in prior to said corpse, in case you missed it."

He stuttered then nodded. "I know that now," he said. "I don't have solid proof Checks is involved, but I had to trust my gut about Little Dan. Don't I get points for being right?" Oh, heck no. "I certainly wouldn't put a hit order past Rider Huntington if he thought the younger of the Dans was a problem in the organization." He glanced at me again. "You have me on the cameras from the post office, here that night." Cherise's eyes narrowed, tightened. How did he know that? "Makes sense you checked the surrounding footage. You want to know why I was here?" She nodded, a barely perceptible motion. "I was following that girl. You know, the waitress, Gabriella. She's not who she says she is."

"Carlita Sanchez," Cherise said, cutting his offer of information off with knowledge of her own. "You can do better than that, Atlas."

He sagged, his attempt to give her something failing miserably. Thanks to me, though I wouldn't have put it past the sheriff to know Gabriella was an alias before I told her. "Did you also know she's Rider's girl?"

Well, that was interesting.

"I only hired her two days ago," Ingrid piped up, reminding me she was there. Cherise shifted her focus to the diner owner and though still angry, she pulled back on some of her animosity. I was sure the fact Ingrid hid evidence from her wasn't winning my friend any brownie points either, probably on par at that point with Joe Atlas. "The morning of the opening. My other girl backed out at the last minute, and I was desperate."

I turned to Cherise, mind still going though I stopped physically. "Could she have left the bag?" But why?

The sheriff nodded once, pivoting toward me. "She could have stolen it," she said. "Betrayed Huntington, taken off. Thought Wallace was a safe place to hide. Except he followed her here." Cherise spoke directly to me, ignoring the other two people present. "If Carlita panicked, she might have stashed it here for the short term."

"Long enough to convince her boyfriend she didn't have it," I said. "Maybe that's why he was here that night."

"If so," Cherise said, "if she convinced him then returned for it, she might have been looking for the bag when Big Dan showed up. Panicked, locked him in the freezer and ran."

"Does Gabriella have keys?" I asked Ingrid directly, using the girl's fake name so as not to confuse the poor woman who was obviously still shaken and staring at me as if she barely knew her own.

"No," Ingrid said. "Just me, I told you that."

"Could she have gotten access to them?" Cherise dropped her arms from her typical dominating cross, her visible softening having a positive influence on Ingrid who thought about it a moment.

"Maybe," she said. "I don't lock them up or anything."

"Which means she could have copied them and returned them and no one would know," I said.

Cherise had visibly relented, her own hands on her hips much like Joe Atlas as she turned to him. "The rest of what you know," she said. "I want everything, no holding back. Or you're going back to Bangor in cuffs."

I'd give him kudos for bravery because he nodded, but with a caveat. "Only if I get my evidence back for helping you solve the murder."

I honestly thought she might snap. Saw her jaw jump, the twitch in her shoulders. Tensed to pull her back—wishful thinking, I know—if she decided to react instead of think. Sighed internally a giant relieved phew of all things *holy that was close* when she nodded abruptly.

"Deal," she snarled. "But if you cross me again, Atlas…" she left that hanging while the detective stuck out his hand and shook hers with a wince.

I'd have hated to be on the other end of that deal.

CHAPTER SIXTEEN

Cherise and Joe Atlas left together, my sheriff friend in possession of the bag. I made sure to follow Ingrid home, though she waved me off when I tried to go inside with her.

"I'm going to lie down," she promised me after a long hug. "Thank you, Seph. I know I made a terrible mistake, but you're right. Dan wasn't supposed to be there that night. I feel terrible he got mixed up in this, but I didn't kill him, did I?" Her pleading gaze and continuing trembling had me gently reassuring her and realizing I shouldn't have let her drive even the handful of blocks to her home, almost insisting I go inside with her regardless, but instead waving to her after one more desperate hug on her part as she finally went inside and closed the door.

Yikes. What a day and it wasn't over yet.

I stopped at the liquor store (don't judge me) to pick up some gin, knowing a drink was in order that evening and maybe even two. When I emerged and headed for my car, I took note of the young man on the corner in the yellow hoody and white sneakers, Checks Johnson speaking to another young man, the pair exchanging something in a quick touch of hands before the other kid hurried off.

Checks looked up as I approached but made no move to leave, eyeing the bottle of gin in my hand, even as I questioned what I was thinking and doing my best not to grasp the glass container like a weapon.

"You're that shrink lady who works with the cops," he said, leaning against the wall, clearly not threatened in the least by little old me, snarky smirk the kind that made adults want to smack kids his age for their arrogance and attitude problem.

"Persephone Pringle," I said, with a nod. "Checks Johnson, right? Though, I assume you have a real first name your mother gave you."

He scowled, turned his head. "Beat it, shrink lady," he said. "Don't need your kind of trouble. Besides, you're bad for business."

Normally, I wouldn't have pushed my luck, turned and walked away, wouldn't have found myself in this position in the first place. But whether it was my lack of sleep or lingering concern about the girls and Trent or worry for Ingrid, irritation at Joe Atlas, remaining thrumming nerves thanks to Billy Abrams, or the fact Cherise rubbed off on me, I simply wasn't going to take that kind of comeback from a punk-ass kid like Checks.

Nope. *Not*.

"If you had something to do with the death of Little Dan Abrams," I snarled, "you think Billy will forgive you for keeping it from him?" That got his attention, Checks whipping his head around, unusual amber eyes huge in surprise. "He gave you a job, didn't he? Likely when no one else would?"

He shifted positions, standing, shoulders slumping, no longer in that casual confrontational pose. Instead, he seemed to shrink in on himself somewhat, head down when he replied.

"Billy's a good guy," he said. "I feel bad for letting him down. But construction work's not my thing."

"I guess selling drugs is more your style," I said. Thought about it a second. "Was Billy involved with that trade along with his brother?"

His reaction had me dismissing the idea

before he even spoke, shock and then rejection on his face. "No way, man," he said. "Billy's mom had all that trouble with prescription drugs when she was sick. And his sister OD'd. Everybody knows, he hates drugs."

"So just Little Dan then," I said.

Checks shrugged just a little. "Listen, I ain't got nothing to do with Big Dan dying, lady, or Little Dan, neither. Truth is, that freaking Rider Huntington *suh*," he added a faint accent to the word that implied derision, "needs to mind his own and go back to his territory before something bad happens."

As if someone like Checks had the chutzpah to threaten Huntington. "You implying Rider had something to do with the Abrams and their deaths?" He didn't respond, but he didn't deny it, either. "What were you doing outside the diner after hours the night Big Dan died?"

"I use that alley regular," he said. "Shortcut home." He pushed off from the wall, clearly ready to leave. "I work at the bowling alley some nights."

Oh, I'd be checking into those fine details. Correction, Cherise would while I learned to mind my own business. "You see Big Dan that night? See anything? Someone maybe messing around with the back door?"

Checks pulled his hood up over his curls, turning away from me. "I didn't see nothing," he said. "Tell the sheriff I got nothing to do with any of it. She wants a killer, ask Rider Huntington some of these here questions and leave me be."

I could have gone after him, badgered him further. Or called a deputy to arrest the kid, search him for drugs. Instead, I returned to my car and texted Cherise. Because Checks was small fish and not going anywhere. The sheriff could deal with him another time. More and more I found myself thinking we might be right about Carlita Sanchez and that, if what Checks suggested was true, the young woman might be in a lot of danger.

And that Rider Huntington had some serious questions to answer.

CHAPTER SEVENTEEN

Naturally, I couldn't leave well enough alone, returning home to do a little digging into Rider Huntington myself. It was rapidly apparent from his open social media and tagged photos and videos he chose parties, beautiful girls in bikinis not to mention fast cars over actually being a productive member of polite society, enough newspaper articles mentioning him being released from custody after a pair of car accidents that ended in him walking away while one of the other drivers didn't and would never walk again proof enough his father had the kind of sway with the local judiciary and law enforcement in Bangor any attempt to bring Rider Huntington to justice was met with the kind of money that made such crimes go away.

As for the girl calling herself Gabriella Torres, it was easy enough to spot her in pics with Rider, though she was never named. Not that it mattered, Carlita Sanchez's identity now confirmed thanks to Joe Atlas.

I was about to go to the kitchen and wash down the terrible taste in my mouth with a glass of gin and cranberry when my phone buzzed. A quick text had me out the door and in the car instead, driving to the sheriff's office.

I need you at the station was all it took because if Cherise was asking, I answered.

The moment I arrived one of the deputies ushered me into a small, dark room with a large glass window, Cherise watching the young woman on the other side of the one-way mirror with her arms crossed and a deep scowl on her face. She nodded to me when I joined her, Carlita Sanchez huddled on the metal chair in the dingy interrogation room, curved in around herself as if positive an attack would come at any moment.

"She's a mess," Cherise said. "I need you to calm her down so I can talk to her."

"Of course," I said. "Has she told you anything I can use?"

Cherise shook her head, gesturing for me to exit, pausing in the hallway outside the interrogation room door. "Just see what you can do," she said.

I wasn't expecting her to let me go in alone and found myself in charge of the suspect in a way that made me as uncomfortable as it did excited. Carlita looked up, huge, dark eyes wide and full of tears, before she half-turned from me, still hugging herself, that miserable slouch a sheer face of resistance I needed to find a way through if I was going to be helpful. Though, to Carlita herself or Cherise or both, I wasn't sure.

Instead of the standard seating, I grabbed the chair on the other side of the table and joined her, sitting next to her, not touching her but close enough she'd know I was there and hopefully not a threat. When she finally looked up again, I let her see my soft smile of sympathy, my hands quiet in my lap, my own posture relaxed.

"Do you remember me, Carlita?" She nodded.

"Ms. Pringle," she said. "Sure."

"I'm a holistic therapist," I said. "And full disclosure, I work with the sheriff sometimes, helping people answer questions when they are upset. Is it okay if we talk?"

She glanced at the door, silent again, lips thinning out as she considered what I'd said. Instead of speaking further now that the legalities were out of the way or choosing to ask any questions, I drew on my training and experience and let her come to me. Watching her unfold a little at a time when it was clear I wasn't there to hurt her satisfied like nothing else, extended silence one of the most powerful tools I'd ever discovered.

"I don't know why I'm here," she finally said. "Ms. Pringle, why was I arrested?" I didn't answer, let her carry on, which she did with increasing volume and a hint of anger. "It's not fair, I didn't *do* anything." Again, I simply sat and listened, nodding just a little, giving her the opening she needed and wanted. "I had nothing to do with that man's death, I swear it." With her insistence came more aggression, more resistance, deeper resentment. "I want to go home."

She fell silent, which meant it was my turn. "Rider won't be happy to find out you're here, will he?" I was taking a leap and a chance that Joe Atlas was right, but figured it was worth the risk considering the information I'd uncovered myself. It paid off instantly, Carlita's anger turning to panic as her gaze flashed to the door, that rigid pose she'd unfurled into collapsing once more. I didn't give her the chance to deny the relationship, carrying on with that same kind and compassionate tone. "Whatever he sent you here to do, Carlita, or if you came here to escape him, I know you did it because you're afraid. Not because you're a bad person."

More tears, giant ones this time, streaming down her face as it contorted, her full lower lip trembling while she choked on air before nodding. "He'll kill me," she whispered in a broken voice. "If he thinks I said anything, I'm dead." But there was more, a hesitation that had me carrying on, this time with a gentle touch to the back of one of her hands as a show of solidarity.

"If he finds out you took the money and drugs," I said.

Carlita shook her head with such violence at that her long ponytail whipped over her shoulder, the breeze it caused carrying the scent of her shampoo cutting through the rather musty smell in the room. "I was here to get it back," she wailed. "He told me to find it and bring it back and not get caught." She crumpled sideways into me, and I caught her, rocking her like I might have a toddler after a particularly scary fall, rubbing her back and letting her weep herself out. When she finally pulled free, I handed her the box of tissues Cherise had left for her and gave her a moment to collect herself before I prodded her again.

"Why did you leave it in the walk-in at the

Grill?" My question was met with shock, confusion, genuine enough in my estimation that guess Cherise and I made had to be wrong.

"It was in the walk-in?" She gaped at me, clutching at the wad of tissues in her hand. "You mean it was there the whole *time*?" Understanding drew a groan from her. "I have no idea how it got there, I swear." Defeat crossed her face, desperate loss. "It was there, and I could have taken it and this would all be over." More crying, Carlita's face reddening under the warm brown of her skin, eyes screwing shut as she stopped breathing in a silent moment of utter despair.

Again, I waited, but worth it, as she returned to me, gasping for breath, rocking herself now until I gently stopped her motion with another touch to her hand.

"Carlita, who took the bag and why did Rider send you to get it?" She might not have been Atlas's thief, but I was positive she had more to say.

"I don't know," she said. "If I knew I'd have taken it back. Rider was punishing me. He's always punishing me."

"For what?" I did everything I could to prove to her I was on her side, from my tone of voice to a soft posture to the empathetic expression I fixed on my face. Not hard to maintain, truth be told. Genuine concern for the young woman who wasn't far off of age from Calliope and Thalia, Carlita's life experience the disadvantage that led her from possibility to probably a prison sentence hit me harder than I was expecting.

Carlita obviously believed my sincerity, because she reached for me this time, hand clasping mine, tugging me closer. "He found out," she whispered, voice thick with tears. "That I loved Danny." She blinked at me while my mind flinched. She was in love with Big—

Oh.

Well, now.

"Little Dan Abrams," I said. "You were a couple?"

She nodded, dabbing at her nose and cheeks with the wad of tissues, her thick mascara tracking down her face in long ribbons of grief. "I was supposed to be Rider's girl, but he has so many, and Danny was sweet. He wasn't like the other guys who Rider shared us with."

Um. Gross. Just—

Rider Huntington hit rock bottom in that moment. And if it was the last thing I did on this blue marble of spinning rock and water, I was going to make sure that particular stain on our planet met the justice he deserved.

I had to inhale slowly, exhale through my parted lips to keep my spike of anger and what she endured from ruining the moment. Except, when she realized how furious I was, Carlita's own expression elevated from utter sorrow to a brief ray of shining hope. That I believed her? Wanted to help her? How little support and kindness had this poor child had her whole life a stranger's reaction to how she'd been treated meant trust and connection?

"Rider found out about you two," I said, the struggle to keep my voice level and kind one of the hardest fights of my life. "Carlita, do you think he killed Danny because of it?"

She didn't say so out loud, but her sink back into mourning and the way her entire being seemed to recoil from that question told me not only did she think so, there was more.

"The night Danny died," she said, surprising me by speaking up when I was sure she was done talking, "he told me he was on an unscheduled pickup, was called on at the last minute, someone else's route. That he'd meet me after he was done with his delivery. But he never came back." She caught her breath, hiccupped through the sob trying to control her, swallowed down her grief and managed to go on. "I found out the next morning he was killed." She licked her lips, blew her nose, jaw setting as though the speaking of it gave her confidence, finally unburdening herself relieving some of the anxiety and horror she'd carried with her since his death. "I was sure Rider had him killed. Why else would he have Danny take a last-minute job? Except." She sighed deeply, body relenting under all that strain, shoulder sagging forward and her chin dropping while doubt crept in. "Danny's delivery. It went missing." She looked up again, confusion returned. "If Rider killed him, where did the package go?"

"You're sure it really disappeared, and Rider didn't make it look like a robbery?" I was positive she had to have thought of that herself, watched it register in her eyes when she nodded.

"He hurt a lot of people after that theft," she said. "If it was a show, he committed."

"I assume he has his own bosses," I said. "Could he have stolen from them and blamed it on a thief?" From what little I knew of Rider I wouldn't put anything past him, and I was positive the more I did get to know him the less I'd doubt he wouldn't sell his own mother if it meant he'd get ahead.

"It's possible," she said, but hesitantly enough she wasn't fully convinced. "Three more packages have gone missing this year.

The one I came to Wallace for was the fifth."

"And you have no idea who stole any of them?" The cynical face of young Checks Johnson flashed in my mind while she shrugged delicately, her tears drying up.

"All Rider said was to come to Wallace and find his merchandise," she said. "He's been punishing me ever since Danny died, but he said this was my chance to make it up to him." Carlita's panic surfaced in a flash as she sat back from me suddenly. "He'll never forgive me now." Another desperate sob wracked her body while she tipped forward, eyes squeezed shut, mouth wide open in a silent expression of terror that had me firmly shaking her to get her to breathe.

"Carlita." I had her attention, her focus, but barely, the young woman's fear overwhelming her. "How did Rider know to come to Wallace?"

Her lips parted several times before she managed a hoarse answer. "He was the one who took the bag from that cop," she said. "Was all pumped about it, went on about how easy it was to bribe the staties and get his property back." So, Rider got his hands dirty and put Joe Atlas in this position, all with the help of another officer. Unless Rider betrayed Atlas, former partners, and the man I was trying to trust was as dirty as I'd feared.

That was a question for later. Because Rider taking personal responsibility left him open for prosecution. Either stupid or brave or both, since so far there had been nothing to pin to him. Why take the risk? Arrogance, more than likely.

"He went to another drop-off, left it in the back," she went on. "Someone broke into his SUV and took it." She shuddered, relaxed again, though that gripping terror could return at any time, I was sure. "He had a camera in the hatch, saw some guy in a dark hoody open the back and take the package. But he said there was no clear view of the guy's ride. Just a logo on the back of his sweatshirt, something to do with Wallace."

Now, who did I know from Wallace who loved hoodies?

CHAPTER EIGHTEEN

Okay, jumping to conclusions, I know. While Checks Johnson had a penchant for that kind of attire, so did a lot of young people in town. Still, hard not to draw a parallel, right? Especially since Little Dan was from right here in Wallace.

"Is Checks Johnson connected to Rider, Carlita?" This might all be over with if she had the right answers.

Instead, she shook her head. "I don't think so, but I don't know for sure." She sniffled, wiped her nose with the tissues in her hand. "I didn't know what to do when I got here, so I talked to Checks, but he wouldn't say anything, though he did tell me Danny had a brother. So, I made friends with Billy, to see if he knew anything."

Smart girl. "And did he?"

"Not from what he told me." She wiped at the last of her tears, setting aside the clump of used tissues stained with her mascara. "I was lost. I had no idea where to look for the package, none. And Billy's clean, never worked for Rider, had nothing to do with business as far as I could tell. I took the job at the Grill to buy myself some time, do some eavesdropping on locals. But I was starting to think Rider was wrong. Until he showed up in town himself."

No wonder she was afraid. "Was that the first time you'd seen him here? The night Big Dan died?"

Carlita nodded. "I wasn't expecting him, didn't know what to do. He cornered me at one point, threatened me. I was so afraid. Then I ran into you in the kitchen, I thought you knew everything." The mishap with the dishes. No wonder she lost it. She wasn't so much inexperienced at the job Ingrid hired her for, she was terrified. "I ID'd the vice detective pretty quick, so I had that to give to Rider, at least." So much for Joe Atlas's attempt to remain undercover. "Rider didn't seem all that surprised."

"Any chance the vice detective is working with your boss?" I almost held my breath waiting for her reply.

"I don't know," she said. "Like I said, he claims he has insiders, paid them off. But why would that cop be here if he was working for Rider?"

Okay, no smoking gun.

Carlita twisted her fingers together and squeezed hard enough her knuckles whitened. "Dirty or not, he was my only chance. He was working here so I decided to stay and see if he'd lead me to the package." She'd begun to tremble, weeping done but fear far from expelled.

"Do you think Rider killed Big Dan?" What motivation could he possibly have had? Was he looking for Joe Atlas, maybe, and stumbled on the dead man, left him in the walk-in? So many connections still unmade.

"I don't know," she said. "But I did see Rider outside the diner when I went back looking for the detective. Not in the alley, though." Carlita tossed her hands in her lap. "The vice cop was my last chance, so I did my best to tail him." She paused one more time, then blurted her last bit of information. "I saw Big Dan go inside." Finally, a possible witness to what actually happened. "But the back door was already open, and there was no one else around. I heard voices, angry voices, didn't want to get caught. So, I ran but I heard the door slam shut behind me, then footsteps running the other direction. I was so scared whoever it was saw me." She met my eyes with her huge brown ones. "Was that the killer?"

I didn't tell her yes because it seemed unnecessary to scare her further despite wishing she'd turned around at the last moment. For all I knew, if she had she'd be dead, too. "Carlita, I need you to tell all of this to the sheriff. Can you do that?"

Her flash into denial hit rebellion in about a staggered heartbeat, her head shaking and whipping hair all the response I needed. Though surely, she had to understand she'd been monitored this entire time, I'd told her as much.

"I already told you he'll kill me," she said, voice humming low with that terror I could only imagine she lived with as a constant companion. "I won't testify against him. And I'll deny anything I said to you." She looked up at the one-way mirror, finally realizing, I suppose, I'd meant what I'd said. Carlita closed down once and for all, turning her head away from me. "I'm a fool. You don't care about me. I'm done."

"One last question," I said while she pinched her lips together, arms crossing over her chest, false bravado doing nothing to disguise her continuing dread. "Do you have a set of keys to the Grill?"

There was confusion again, a head shake. "Ingrid had the only set," she said.

And that, it seemed, was that.

I emerged from interrogation to find Cherise exiting the viewing room, her lovely face creased in a frown.

"Without her testimony, I can't do much about Rider," she said.

"I'm not sure he was responsible for Big Dan anyway," I said, "though if he did kill Little Dan out of revenge and kept the stolen product for himself, there's a good chance his bosses would disapprove." Drug cartels weren't exactly known for their compassion and understanding. "But she's right about one thing. Why go to such lengths to make examples of others if he took the stuff himself? And why put himself into a compromising position by retrieving his property from Detective Atlas unless he had something to prove to his employers?"

Cherise nodded. "It's much more likely someone killed Little Dan and stole his merch," she said. "While one or two thefts are possibly unconnected, a string of five over one year feels like someone's targeting Rider's distribution network. Someone with inside information."

"Someone who sells drugs himself on street corners?" I hated to finger Checks Johnson, but the kid was hardly an angel. "Checks was working with Billy," I said, "and could have stolen Ingrid's keys long enough to make copies. If he was the one in the hoody who took the bag from Rider's car, it's possible he stashed it in the walk-in as a temporary measure then got fired and couldn't return to retrieve it." And yet, if he was right and he walked past that alley every night, what stopped him?

Cherise, however, carried on. "It's possible he left it there to give himself time to figure out what to do with it. The diner was still closed after all, and he may not have known when Ingrid meant to open. He may have miscalculated and went back to the diner to retrieve it that night when he realized his mistake."

"Carlita said the door was already open." Which meant that Checks might have ducked inside, and Big Dan saw him do it. Went after him because he'd been there to break in anyway and the two arguing voices the young woman had heard were theirs.

"Dan was a big guy," Cherise said, doubt creeping in. "Checks not so much." Agreed.

The kid was tall, but a skinny whip while Big Dan had the presence of a wall of stone. "Still, if Checks was already in the walk-in and Dan caught him there, Checks could have been fast enough to slip around him, shut the door to keep him from following."

This was making more and more sense to me, though I couldn't stop the nagging feeling I was missing something. "Which means Big Dan's death was accidental. Checks likely had no intent to kill him, just save himself."

"If the final report says Big Dan died from complications due to the walk-in," Cherise said, "it's still manslaughter at the very least, Seph."

Fair enough, and a tragic mistake that would no doubt ruin the young man's life and any chance he might have had to turn himself around.

The worst kind of ending.

"And Rider?" Surely, she was planning to talk to him?

She shrugged, frustration showing in the abruptness of that motion. "He was here already," she said. "Came in without me having to ask. Brought four lawyers with him." Ah. Now her irritation with Carlita's reticence was understandable. "I can't touch him without something solid and I've got nothing."

"What happens to Carlita now?" I tried not to feel bad for the young woman and her own terrible choices as I followed Cherise through the bullpen and to the exit.

"I'm not holding her," she said, "but the FBI have questions so as soon as they arrive, she's out of my hands." She hugged me quickly, let me go. "Thanks, Seph. I know you probably feel guilty about getting her to talk, but you did her a favor. She has to face what she's done in order to rehabilitate."

I knew that, left with a wave, a little guilt lingering nonetheless because I was usually on the other side when it came to my job. While the frustration Rider Huntington might get away with the murder of Little Dan because his so-called girlfriend, a desperate, vulnerable and manipulated young woman out of options, got to live in terror she'd get the same treatment.

There had to be something I could do to make sure he met justice.

Yeah, because confronting a known drug dealer with a tendency to kill those who got in his way while escaping the law thanks to his father's money was a brilliant life decision.

Why then was that exactly the plan I had in mind?

CHAPTER NINETEEN

He wasn't that hard to find, the expensive sports car parked in the lot at the local bar more than enough indication I'd found the young man in question. I didn't go looking, I swear, driving past all it took to catch my attention and prod me to hit the brakes. At least he had the good taste to choose black instead of lime green or some variation of yellow or red that screamed dudebro. Still, the pretentiousness of the extravagant vehicle taking up two spaces—one of them clearly marked disabled—marked Rider Huntington's location like a waving flag.

Of course, by the time I parked my own SUV and climbed out, I was second, third and twenty-guessing my decision to talk to him without Cherise or any kind of backup. It wasn't like the trust fund kid from Bangor turned drug kingpin was going to just blurt out a confession or anything. From what Joe Atlas said, he'd been clever enough up to this point to keep himself out of prison despite being brought in for questioning on a number of occasions.

Telling myself I was only doing recon, that a single drink imbibed at the bar observing Rider Huntington was all I would risk and knowing I was lying to myself, I headed into Maverick's Bar past the bouncer in black who nodded to me after giving me the once over.

I had never set foot inside this particular establishment before, the previous incarnation a family restaurant, so the dim interior and thudding music was a bit of an adjustment compared to my memory of chintzy décor and smiling waitresses. Instead, a young woman in a slinky black dress gave me that same up and down the bouncer did before gesturing at the nearly empty bar with a bored and detached expression on her overly-made-up face.

It wasn't a seat I was looking for, however, noting a small area in the back elevated by a few steps, cordoned off with an iron railing, a semi-circle of what looked like velvet upholstered sofas circling a center table guarded by another black-clad bouncer.

And who else was seated on that exact sofa with his arm around a skinny young woman in a barely-there dress? None other than Rider Huntington himself.

My feet moved without my consent, carrying me toward the VIP area and up to the bouncer before I could come up with a good reason for being there, the bulky body-builder who really needed to back off the steroids if he planned to have kids one day blocking my advance with those pumped-up biceps bulging as he folded his arms over his chest in that universal go away stance that needed nothing else to be intimidating.

Except, I'd come this far and, with a tiny (okay, more than tiny) thrill of excited fear stirring in my stomach, I leaned around tall, broad and brooding. "Rider."

He looked up, head tilting to one side, lazy smile fixed on me though it took him a moment before he waved for me to join him. Curiosity was a powerful tool, I knew, and I'd clearly piqued his.

The bouncer stepped aside, exposing the fact Rider didn't need him if the two tall, dark-suited bodyguards who flanked the sofa were there to protect him. Now firmly outnumbered, I took those three wide steps to the platform where the handsome, suited and self-possessed target of my interest lounged back, smirk firmly in place, his slow gaze traveling my person in a way that offended far more than the previous two experiences had.

"Do I know you?" He leaned forward to retrieve his drink, what looked like scotch in a short glass lifted to his full lips in a slow and languid motion. You know, he really was attractive, or would have been if a shark didn't live behind his blue eyes, a predator doing nothing to hide in that smile, his posture, the way his gaze lingered on me as though wondering if I was good to eat.

"Persephone Pringle," I said, struggling not to touch my hair, adjust my black leather motorcycle jacket, shift my feet, holding still and forcing calm confidence on the outside. Any move, any adjustment, would show weakness. "I'm a therapist." His eyebrows twitched at that. "I work with the sheriff's department." Now, you may think telling him that might have been a bad idea, but I guessed otherwise. See, someone like Rider Huntington had a deep-seated need to be noticed, appreciated, even for his wrongdoing. Maybe even more so than anything else. And presenting with an opportunity to taunt someone in law enforcement, even as peripherally as me, was a lure I knew he'd never be able to pass up.

As long as I could keep him talking, he might actually give me something I could use. Or, at the very least, share with Cherise so she could act.

Yes, I was fully aware how stupid this was, but the train had left the station and I could either steer it or jump. Chose to sit though I wasn't invited, leaning back, crossing my legs, giving him silence while his smile deepened before he spoke.

"Darling, give us a minute." The girl rose, left with a pout, while my own smile rose unbidden, my experience with men like him serving me after all. "A therapist," he said then, saluting me with his drink. "Didn't I see you at that diner the other night?" He didn't miss much.

"Yes," I said. "It turns out you were having a conversation with someone I know. A young man named Checks."

Rider's grin tightened. "An entrepreneurial soul," he said. "I salute such endeavors."

My confidence continued to increase as I settled into the conversation, all his cues familiar, his attitude nearly textbook. Free of empathy, deluded that money would protect him forever, it was actually harder to take him seriously than it was to hang onto my composure. Rider Huntington might have thought he was the king of all he surveyed, but until he proved otherwise, I had the distinct feeling it wouldn't take much to burst his little balloon.

I just needed leverage.

"I understand you two share business interests," I said.

Rider shrugged, long, lean body at rest but his mind not, the visible reactions across his handsome face showing me tell after tell that would make him someone simple to swindle at poker. I suppose he'd never had to learn to hide who he really was, money and entitlement all the endearing qualities he needed to make it in life. So far.

We'd see how well they served him against me.

"Let's cut to the reason you're here," he said, leaning forward with his elbows on his knees, the clear threat of his sudden movement unexpected so soon, but then again, his lack of age and experience hadn't yet taught him the subtler forms of intimidation which only calmed me further while I read him like a book.

"Of course," I said. "I need you to confess to murdering Dan Abrams." Paused, thought about it a moment while his eyes widened. "Both of them."

Rider's shock was so real in that instant I almost tsked in response. It had to be genuine. I hadn't given him a chance to soften his reaction. He did finally chuckle, finishing his drink, clicking his fingers for another before motioning to me with his glass, the invitation to join him obvious. I waved away the offer, smiling back at him while he pondered my question with narrowed eyes.

"If you had any evidence against me for either crime," he said, "the sheriff and I would be talking via my lawyers right now."

"If you say so." I let him chew on that a moment. "Do your bosses know how much of their product and money you've lost over the last year, Rider? Or have you been covering it up so they don't do to you what you did to Danny Abrams?"

Rider's face tightened, the shark surfacing. "You have no idea what you're talking about."

"Oh, I think I do." Was it wrong this was fun? I really needed my head examined because yes, it was, and I shouldn't have been there without Cherise, and I wasn't a cop and what was I even thinking? Carried on regardless. "Though, killing off your own people and stealing from your employers doesn't sound like the best way to extend your lifespan."

Rider spluttered. I had him off guard,

pushed harder while the two men in dark suits who stood guard exchanged a look that told me even if I was wrong, young Master Huntington was going to have some fast talking to do very shortly. Because they didn't work for him, did they?

Apparently not.

"You can deny Danny worked for you," I said, "and you can threaten your people, punish them while helping yourself to product and profits. You can even avoid prison. But when those who use you to sell drugs find out you've been stabbing them in the back..." I let that hang. Knowing now it wasn't true, that Rider had nothing to do with the thefts and I'd possibly set him up for a very messy end.

For that, I was honestly sorry. Mostly. Kind of. Squeaked some empathy out.

I was a therapist, not a saint.

"How about I throw you a bone," he snarled, sliding to the edge of the sofa, so close our knees touched, finally deciding to show his teeth. "Since you're hot and all, for a cougar." Yeah, that bought him no respect whatsoever. "I had nothing to do with Danny Abrams dying. He did work for me, yes, running merchandise." His perfect veneers flashed. "You know, my legit business dealings. I had no reason to kill him, least of all to steal from myself." His head tilted just a little, and was that a nervous glance at the men in the suits who guarded him? My assumption they didn't work for Rider was confirmed with that look. "But if I was a cop? I'd be asking if someone right here in good old Wallace might have a reason to kill both Dans. Like that vice undercover who's gotten himself into trouble. Or the freelancer we have in common."

Rider might have been deflecting, but his suggestion Little Dan's death had something to do with his father's, outside of Rider himself, had me thinking. Joe Atlas wasn't squeaky clean even if he wasn't on the take, but could he be the killer, in deep even before he went undercover? His other reference came through loud and clear. Checks Johnson's mention could be an attempt to set the kid up. On the other hand, I'd already come to believe Rider wasn't responsible for either death. Selling drugs, being a scumbag and a general jerkface? You better believe it. But a murderer? Not in these two cases at least.

"Now," Rider said, standing and buttoning his jacket, tossing back the full drink he'd just been handed by the young woman I'd displaced, "if you'll excuse me, I'm going to go report to my lawyers that the Wallace Sheriff's Department tried to interrogate me without them present."

I watched him go, caught the glance back from one of the bodyguards, scowling after the punk and hoping I didn't get Cherise in trouble. Waited until they were gone before heading out myself, climbing into my SUV and slamming the door. Right before squeaking in surprise and a surge of fear as the passenger's side opened and Joe Atlas jumped in.

"That was dumb," he said. "Get anything interesting?"

I snort laughed, mostly from the outlay of adrenaline. "It *was* dumb," I said. "Rider didn't kill either Dan."

"You're sure?" Joe's face settled into frustration, glaring out the windshield at the front of the building though not seeing it from the way he chewed his lower lip, squinting as though his mind turned. "That leaves Checks Johnson then."

"Rider seemed to think you might have motive," I said, the detective's returned snort authentic enough in its humor I wasn't buying the trust fund kid's attempt at deflection either. "You do realize Carlita made you, right?" Joe's gaze flashed to me, eyes widening. "You're part of the reason Rider is in Wallace in the first place. She outed you."

The detective's swearing ended abruptly,

with a firm punch to my dash. "That's it, then," he said, sinking into the seat. "I'm burned and I'll probably lose my shield over this." Joe groaned. "What a mess, Atlas." He fished out his phone, cueing up a video. "At least I have this to prove I'm clean."

He showed me the clip, of what looked like a dashcam from a cruiser, Rider Huntington shaking hands with a young cop in uniform, the bag exchanged between them.

"Hopefully, my bosses will at least take this into consideration before they can me," he said. "And that your sheriff will believe me now I'm not dirty."

My phone vibrated, text from Cherise reminding me I had my own troubles to worry about. *Get your butt to the station RIGHT NOW.*

Um. Whoops. I guess Rider Huntington wasn't bluffing and Joe Atlas wasn't the only one about to get his rear end kicked into next week.

Joe was staring at me when I looked up from the message. I finally relented in the face of his regret, solidarity in our mutual trouble hard to dispel.

"I'll try to convince Cherise to help you if you help us," I said, pretty sure it was an empty promise at this point, but he'd already withheld information twice so if I couldn't help because she was as furious with me as she'd been with him, I wouldn't feel all that badly about failing in the effort. When I fired up the engine, Joe immediately reached for his seatbelt. "But if you keep anything from us that could put this investigation at risk…"

He shook his head, spreading both hands out in front of him like a promise.

One I bought. For now.

CHAPTER TWENTY

Cherise wasn't in the bullpen or her office when I arrived with Joe, a deputy guiding me instead to the observation room and leaving us there. This time I stood on the other side of the glass, observing as Cherise spoke with Checks. Joe leaned against the sill of the one-way mirror, gaze intent on the young man in the yellow hoody. It wasn't lost on me the only reason he was even in here with me was because I brought him with me, something I really hoped I didn't come to regret but couldn't help gnawing around the edges of as Checks denied everything.

"We searched your place, Checks," she said. "Found a pair of keys. Turns out they open the back door of the diner." And checkmate. Sadly, since I actually was rooting for the kid. "Mind telling me where you acquired them if you had nothing to do with Big Dan's death?" Cherise hadn't warned me ahead of time she'd found evidence or even officially arrested Checks which meant that angry text put me in her black book, hopefully only temporarily. Regardless, I was here for his reaction, to give her what I discovered, and I wasn't going to fail her by letting Joe Atlas's presence—or my screwup with Rider—distract me.

Checks scowled at the small keyring in the plastic bag, pushing it away from him, sitting back with his arms crossed and glaring. "I found them," he said. "On my way home the other night. Figured someone lost them so I took them. You know, to return them to the rightful owner."

Sure, he had. More likely he'd have spent the next few weeks trying it out on people's doors to see if he could liberate their belongings, but I wasn't judging.

Cherise slowly pushed it back toward him while he turned his head and refused to look. "You were there that night," she said. "I have you on a security feed, Checks. So, what happened, you broke into the diner looking to score and Big Dan caught you?"

Checks wiped at his upper lip with the cuff of his hoody, visible signs of agitation making me frown. Not guilt, but fear. "I told you, I walk that alley every night on my way home. I never saw nothing, and I didn't go inside. I found those keys," he poked at the bag, "at the end of the alley. So, whoever you're looking for, they be clumsy or something and left it behind."

Likely story, and pretty thin, though Cherise had to have confirmed he'd been seen multiple evenings on the post office feed using the alley. Or why else would he even suggest it as any kind of alibi? His nervousness aside, I could have been reading him wrong, his anxiety not fear after all but regret.

Whatever my input, it seemed Cherise had what she needed, the sheriff standing and taking the bag with her as she approached the door. Paused to confront Checks one more time, classic police tactic for impact.

"It'll go easier on you if you confess, Checks," she said, "but I have enough evidence to put you away for the death of Dan Abrams and I assure you, that's exactly what I'm going to do." She closed the door, leaving him alone.

Checks immediately squirmed in place, his panic flashing over his face. And denial. Pure, unadulterated, fear-fed denial.

And despite the evidence to the contrary, I believed him.

Not what Cherise wanted to hear, trust me, and neither, it turned out, did Joe Atlas, though I knew his motivation for a quick wrap-up leaned to the self-serving.

"You got your guy," he said the moment Cherise opened the door to the observation room. "I need my evidence back."

"You'll get it," she said, "when I'm done with it. Which will be after Checks goes down for manslaughter. And you get cleared by your handler."

Joe's rising frustration ended in him stomping out of the room while I winced and met the sheriff's eyes, her own expression turning from satisfied to irritated.

"Joe's clean," I blurted. "I saw a video of Rider with the cop he bribed to steal the merch." Took a breath. "And Checks didn't do it."

She sighed, jaw jumping. Shook the keys in the bag at me. "He did, Seph. And it's possible he had something to do with the younger Abrams's death, too. And the thefts."

Bet she was regretting asking for my input now, huh? "It's possible," I said. "But I believe him."

"Good thing I'm sheriff, then," she said, stepping aside. "Oh, and next time you decide to interrogate a suspect without telling me first and interfering with an investigation that puts my work in jeopardy? Don't." She seemed to hesitate, relenting just a little. "It's all on me, but stay clear of Rider Huntington, please. Thanks for the help, really." Why did I get the impression it was the last time she'd ask? "Go home."

I could have stayed and argued with her. Contemplated it. Caught the steady and steadfast resistance in her eyes and knew I'd lose, likely not just the argument but possibly my friendship. And chose to trust her.

She was the law, after all. And I'd been known to make mistakes.

Why then did I struggle with accepting abandoning Checks Johnson wasn't one of them? Sure, the kid was guilty of something, but killing Big Dan? I wasn't buying it.

Went home anyway, dusk fading to darkness, a text from Trent landing as I parked in my driveway.

Sorry I missed you, he sent. *Was in DC. Let me know when you have time for that talk.*

Argh. Like I wanted to deal with this right now? Not.

Instead, I went inside, tossing my bag and my jacket and stomping to the kitchen to pour myself a gin, switching on the light over the stove and shutting it off again when I was done. For some reason, I preferred the dark right about now. Headed to my office and sank into my chair, Belladonna jumping up and promptly chirping at me for dinner.

I'd forgotten to shut down my web browser, Rider Huntington's social media still on my screen, making me even crankier. But, as I jiggled my mouse to close it, something caught my attention and I clicked without thinking.

To another profile, with two young men, wearing identical hoodies, both with small Wallace High logos over their hearts. Hoodies I'd seen all around town for years because the school never changed their design, the deep blue and silver lettering, while not visible in the photo of smiling faces, nonetheless etched into my memory.

I had one myself in my dresser, Calliope's an extra-large on baggy purpose she still wore sometimes.

And the word WALLACE crossed the back of every single one.

Never mind the logo one of them used as his profile picture, a logo I'd seen on a discarded sign behind The Blueberry Grill, already knew tied him to the diner, to the reno. But only then, at that moment, binding everything together.

I knew who stole the drugs. Possibly why. The question was, did that same person have anything to do with the deaths of both Dans?

CHAPTER TWENTY-ONE

Belladonna pawed at me, her need for dinner outweighing everything, in her opinion. Though, as I stood to do her bidding, knowing I had to call Cherise and wondering the best way to make that happen, I exited the office and headed for the main house.

Even as my cat, her eagerness for supper typically all-consuming, stopped in her tracks. Stared into the dark kitchen.

And hissed.

"I never meant to hurt anyone," he said, stepping out of the shadows, the gun in his shaking hand belying his words. Billy Abrams ran the other through his messy hair, gesturing for me to join him, Belladonna slinking behind me while I raised both hands, heart speeding up, though not as much as it should have. Not like this was the first time my life had been threatened, and by more dangerous people than him. But there was a desperate horror on his face, more visible as I drew nearer, that had me worried he might not intend to shoot me, but one false move could make that trembling trigger finger do the deed despite his desires.

"Billy," I said, sitting at the peninsula when he pointed at the stool with the muzzle of his gun. "You don't have to do this." Wow, I sounded like every Hollywood actress who always got shot after saying the stupidest thing possible to the gunman.

"I don't have a choice," he said, teeth chattering together, tall body rigid as he fought for control of himself. I felt Belladonna leap up behind me, heard the soft sound of her paws on the counter, wished she'd make a run for it. Bad enough if he hurt me, but if she somehow was shot or killed, I'd never forgive myself.

If I was even around to do any forgiving.

"Billy," I said, holding out both hands in that universal sign of weaponless compliance, "what happened to your father, it was an accident. Wasn't it?"

He twitched, moaned softly, half-turning away from me, that free hand in his hair again, pacing in short bursts of energy doing nothing to make me feel less threatened. "It wasn't supposed… he shouldn't have been…" Billy stopped, shook the gun at me. "I never meant it to happen like this."

"I know," I said, softly, soothing as best I could with my own voice shaking. "I know, Billy. It's going to be okay."

And that was possibly the single worst thing I could have said to him, his barking laugh of fury and rejection met with another shake of the gun. "It's not!" His voice cracked when he shouted those words, entire body vibrating. "It's never going to be okay ever again."

Careful, Persephone. Think before you speak. "You could have walked away," I said. "They arrested Checks. The sheriff thinks he did it."

Billy shook his head, twisting and turning as though fighting a voice inside him, struggling with a demon he could barely contain. "You don't understand," he wailed. "They found the keys. It's going to come back on me. It's all going to come back on me." His arm lowered, the gun pointing at the ground, a massive sob escaping him. "They'll do a search and find out I made those keys. Why did I do it local?" He slapped himself in the forehead, so hard I jumped at the sound, Belladonna growling low behind me. "I never thought I'd get caught, didn't plan for any of this." Billy met my eyes, his face sheathed in tears, eyes haunted, free hand rising toward me. "You have to understand, I never meant for any of this to happen."

Guilt. The demon was guilt. And there was only one way to purge it. "Tell me," I said, hoping I was right, and that the tactic would work. Otherwise? I'd be his next victim. "Billy, tell me. I can help you."

He stared at me then, body suddenly silent, gun still aimed at the carpet at his feet. "You'll talk to the sheriff for me?"

I nodded immediately. "I can't promise you anything," I said. "Billy, you have to tell the truth. It's the only way you can make up for what's happened."

At first, I wasn't sure I'd made the right move, that offering him redemption was the path he sought. Until he softened, sagging to the other stool, the gun on the counter between us but pointing away. Yes, he still held it, but I no longer feared a random bullet. Now, if I could only convince him to hand it over before he changed his mind about talking instead of shooting.

"That's why you're here," I said, still gentle, understanding, with all the compassion I could muster. "You need to tell someone. You don't want to hurt anyone else, Billy." He shook his head, weeping, leaning forward until his forehead pressed against my shoulder. I held him, let him cry, on the verge of my own tears as the terror of the last few minutes fought to surface. When he finally straightened, he released the gun, pushing it gently toward me, face in shadows, whole soul in darkness.

"I killed my brother last year," he said, voice quiet, composed, the black of the kitchen hiding his expression when he stared down at his hands in his lap. To my shock, Belladonna circled me, approaching Billy. I almost pulled her away, but he looked up, saw her. Reached out and touched her fur. She instantly started to purr, stepping down into his lap and I held back while he cradled her in his arms, finally brave enough myself at her show of trust to slide the gun out of his reach before exhaling a shaking breath.

Gun out of play. Awesome.

Billy took a moment to tend to Belladonna then looked up and met my eyes, peace passing over his face. "I always looked up to him, you know. Until he moved to Bangor and got involved with Huntington." Billy's expression shifted, tightened, judgment and resentment flashing. "We fought about it, about him selling drugs like that. He was Dad's favorite, the oldest. If Dad had found out, he'd have been devastated. But he had no idea." Billy cleared his throat, Belladonna rubbing her forehead against his cheek as she stood and head-butted him for more attention. "I went to see him that night, drove to Bangor to try to talk him into coming home. We had a fight. A dumb fight. He knew how I felt about drugs. About what they did to Mom. To Perry." His mother's prescription addiction, his sister's OD. So tragic, all of his losses, not the least of which the ones he took part in. "It was nothing, we fought before, so many times. But I snapped that night. When he turned his back, with that bag in his hands, I punched him. So hard." Billy's voice cracked, warbled. "He went down. Hit the ground. One punch and he was dead."

"It shouldn't have killed him," I said when he stopped, staring at the floor, horror returning. "It was an accident, Billy." He looked up, swallowing, wiping at his mouth with the cuff of his Wallace High hoody before going back to patting Belladonna in a reflexive rise and fall of his hand. "He had an aneurysm. It could have happened at any time, from any impact."

"But it didn't," he said. "It happened when I hit him."

No arguing his logic when he was lost this deep in regret.

"I grabbed the bag," he said. "I wasn't thinking. I didn't know what else to do so I ran." He bent his head, forehead pressed to Belladonna's for a moment. She licked his cheek and he pulled away, rocking her. "I was going to turn it in, but Danny was dead. I figured the cops would think a rival took it so I brought it to a worksite and got rid of it." He shrugged. "The new bank on Main and Lewis?" I nodded. "It's buried in the foundation."

More and more fell into place. "It wasn't the last time you took from Rider's network," I said.

Billy nodded. "I had to try to make up for it somehow. Took trips to Bangor, followed Rider around, his guys. Wasn't hard. They weren't expecting me most of the time." His jaw jumped. "At least, at first. The last one, I almost got caught."

"Detective Atlas," I said. "The undercover cop?"

Billy wiped his nose again, went back to his endless caress of my purring cat. "I figured at least he had the goods, right? But when I was leaving, I saw Rider get the bag from that dirty cop, put it in his SUV. I had to do something."

"You didn't know he had a camera in the back," I said. Pointed at his hoody. "Or that he'd track you to Wallace."

"Danny never told him about me," he said. "When Rider showed up, I panicked. I knew why he was in town. Looking for the stash. I was sure he was going to kill me."

"Except he didn't know it was you," I said. "Or that you'd hidden the bag in the diner's walk-in." The logo he used in his social media profile was for his reno company. The same logo I'd seen on the sign behind the diner. The company Checks worked for so briefly but didn't own. Nope, he worked for Billy.

The one who'd dropped the keys.

"I knew who Gabriella really was," Billy said. "Danny told me all about her, so when she showed up, I knew I had to find a place to dump the stuff. I stole Ingrid's keys, made a quick copy at the hardware store down the street. It was only supposed to be temporary. I stored the bag in the walk-in, thinking we had another couple of days of construction. Except Ingrid decided to open early and I lost my chance to get it back before she did." He shifted on the stool, face falling, crumpling with grief. "I thought I hid it really well. But she found it somehow. So, when I went back to get it… it was already gone. At first, I thought it was Carlita, that she'd figured it out, but it didn't matter then, because Dad…"

"Your father walked in on you," I said.

"Wanted to know what you were doing there."

"He should have just stayed away!" Billy's outburst had Belladonna sitting up, her purr silenced, her anxiety reaching him when nothing else, it seemed, could. He soothed her with more scratches, the cat settling, while he exhaled a long, shaking breath. "Dad was there to teach Ingrid a lesson," he said, shaking his head. "He never could let anything go. Found me in the walk-in, thought I was there for the same reason. Got all self-righteous on me, even though he was the one who planned to trash the place. We fought." He caught his breath. "We always fought. I pushed him, he tried to hit me, so I slammed the door on him and left. I didn't mean for him to die, I swear. I figured he'd be fine, that they'd find him the next morning. He'd get what was coming to him. But I knew I was screwed. Dad wouldn't have protected me. He'd have told the sheriff I was the one who locked him in. I figured it was all over. The truth would finally come out."

"Except your father had a heart attack," I said.

Billy wept, nodding over and over while rocking Belladonna.

"I need to call the sheriff now," I said. "Billy, you understand that don't you?"

He didn't respond, his story told, silently

holding my cat, and crying without a sound for the five minutes it took for my quiet call for help resulted in Cherise striding through my door.

"You were right," he said to me as she cuffed him and led him out, Belladonna now in my arms. "Talking helped. I feel better. Thank you."

He'd have no idea how long I sat at my kitchen counter after they'd gone, my turn to hug and shake over my purring cat.

CHAPTER TWENTY-TWO

I pulled into the parking lot outside Trent's office, leaving the coffee cup I'd brought from The Blueberry Grill behind, already empty. While the conversation I was about to have with my ex-husband might not have been a pleasant one to look forward to, the one I'd just left had that part of my life sorted, at least.

Cherise forgave me immediately, of course, she did. The sheriff's good humor during our breakfast "meeting" (hello greasy diner food and lots of coffee) and my profuse apology despite the fact she relented in her irritation quickly washed away any lingering doubt our friendship remained solid.

"Just promise me," she'd said over her big breakfast, repeating her plea like she didn't think it got through the first time she said it "the next time you decide to question a suspect, you tell me first."

"Next time?" She would never know the level of relief I felt at those two words. "I'm not fired already?"

She grinned, saluted me with her coffee mug. "Not yet," she winked.

"I heard Carlita is in FBI custody," I said, trying not to drool over her hash browns and caving to take one when she made the offer. Ingrid knew how to run a fryer, the now beamingly happy owner of the hottest place in town no longer a nervous wreck and even fully staffed.

Cherise mopped up some yolk with her toast, nodding. "She's on the hook for fraud charges, but I hear the district attorney offered her a deal. We'll see if she's smart enough to take it. I doubt it. And without her turning state's evidence on his operation, Rider Huntington walks."

For now. Sharks like him tended to go belly up eventually from sheer arrogance.

"Is it true you got Checks in a trades program?" I grinned at her while she sighed and eye rolled.

"Don't start with me," she said. "The kid's got a world of problems he's facing and selling drugs doesn't begin to define them, but he's young and, I think, maybe smart enough to know when he's being offered a golden ticket."

"I hope so," I said.

"If not, he knows any offense means prison instead of learning a real trade." She leaned back from her now empty plate, coffee in hand. "I guess it's up to him now."

"At least someone ended up happy," I said. "You gave Detective Atlas the evidence?"

"Called it a co-operation," she said, nose wrinkling, distaste clear but her choice made. "Convinced his handlers he worked with me instead of whatever that was." She flicked her fingers. "He owes me one."

Maybe not a bad thing in the long run.

"And Billy?" I hadn't wanted to ask but couldn't help myself. My heart still ached for the poor young man who'd lost his entire family, including two to horrible twists of fate he'd blame himself for until the day he joined them.

"I had to hand him over to state, Seph," she said. "At the very least, he's on the hook for destroying evidence of a major crime. And while he may not have purposely killed either his brother or his father, it's going to be up to the DA to decide if he wants to pursue manslaughter charges."

"I get it," I said. "It's just tragic."

"Life's like that sometimes." She checked her phone, waved to Ingrid. "This one's on me." She leaned forward, dark eyes meeting mine. "Oh, and if you could add not dying or putting yourself in the line of fire ever again to that list of things not to do so you keep your job with the department?"

She made me laugh, left after paying the check, while I lingered and thought about the last few days. And made a decision.

Which led me here, to Trent's office on a lovely Monday morning and my resolution not to murder him no matter what he came out with. Because disappointing Cherise instead of working with her? Not an option.

Trent stood when I walked in at the guidance of his receptionist, allowing her to show me the way like I hadn't been here a million times before. It wasn't helping he appeared visibly nervous, not like him. I took the seat across from him while he closed the door and sat behind his desk, hand shuffling papers in front of him, clearing his throat as he adjusted his tie. Not getting to the point.

My job, I suppose. "If you're going to judge our daughter for who she loves," I said, coming out with it because I was tired of having this hanging over me like the shroud of doom it felt like, "I never knew you, I'm ashamed of you and you can just go to hell, Trent Garret."

He blinked at me, eyes widening, shaking his head. "What are you talking about?"

"The fact you asked for this little talk shortly after discovering Calliope and Thalia are a couple," I said. "Don't deny it. I know you saw them at dinner."

Trent sat back in his chair, sorrow crossing his face. "Seph," he said, "I've known they loved each other for over a year now."

Wait. What? I gaped at him, at a loss for words (and that was hard to do, in case you missed it) while he sighed and rubbed at the base of his left ring finger. Where his wedding ring no longer sat.

"I can't believe you'd believe." He stopped, started again. "I love Callie and Thalia and I'm very happy for them. That's not... how could you think that?" The hurt in his face whiplashed me with regret.

"I'm sorry," I said. "I'm very sorry. I just... what then?"

He leaned forward again, sliding a piece of paper toward me. I took it, scanned it, brain not quite comprehending, but that was okay because he told me out loud what my eyes and mind couldn't compute.

"Our daughter quit school," he said. "And didn't tell us about it."

CHAPTER TWENTY-THREE

She... what? That bratty little—

"Wait, how do you know?" I held up the letter, addressed to Calliope, not us. Not Trent. "Where did you get this?" The college admissions officer expressed her regret at Callie exiting her business program and wished her the best. Nope, no mention of me or her father, so why was this in his possession?

Trent had the good grace to wince. "The last time I was over to see her, she mentioned helping Thalia on Friday afternoon, something to do with the greenhouse. But she has accounting on Fridays." He stopped, paling. "Yes, I have her schedule memorized."

"You went behind her back and got this from the college." I shook the page at him. "Trent, she was there on a full-ride scholarship.

There was absolutely no need for them to contact either one of us." Something we'd discuss when I got my hands on her but right now, I was angrier with him for snooping than her for—

Lying to me.

Cherise had better get her handcuffs ready because as soon as I reamed my ex, I was going to murder my kid.

"You're not concerned she quit school?" Oh, how like him, to turn his paranoid delusions and digging into Calliope's personal life around as if he hadn't just broken a sacred trust and invaded our kid's privacy.

She didn't tell me. Why didn't she tell me? She had every chance to—

Dead. She was *dead*.

"Don't change the subject," I snapped, standing and slamming the page down on the desk. "You realize the reason she didn't tell us is probably because you pull this kind of stunt all the time."

He stood, red in the face now, bitterness surfacing though I had to believe a part of him felt guilty. "Someone has to make sure she's safe," he said.

"Trent." I caught the next words I was going to say in favor of not telling him where he could go and take his FBI profiler fears with him. "Do you have any idea how much damage this will do to your relationship with your daughter?"

He hesitated at last. Swallowed hard. As someone knocked then entered with a cheery, "Honey, you forgot your—"

I turned, took in the brunette in the suit, her fading smile, anxiety instead crossing her face as she looked back and forth between us. And made a leap of assumption that really wasn't that huge a jump considering the paper bag in her hand and the implication of her possession of what looked like lunch.

"Persephone Pringle." I stuck out my hand, shook hers despite the limp contact.

"Melanie," she said, still staring at Trent before forcing a smile for me. "Melanie Anderson."

"Nice to meet you." I spun on my ex, totally ignoring his girlfriend—YAY! He really *did* have an honest-to-goodness girlfriend and under other circumstances, I'd make more of an effort—and finished what I had to say. "You'd better think about what you're going to tell Calliope. Just as soon as you apologize to her for letting her think you were judging her and Thalia. And then," I spun and left as I wrapped up, "beg her to forgive you for never minding your own business."

By the time I reached my SUV, I'd discarded my anger for Trent (okay, not entirely) and transferred my attention instead to the young woman I gave birth to who, for some reason I was going to wring from her cold and lifeless body, lied to me. I'd come out and asked her what her father might possibly want to talk to me about. And she *lied*.

Used Thalia and herself as a reason when she knew darned well exactly what Trent had uncovered. Had chances—chances I'd given her on purpose, knowing she had more to share—and *lied*.

And here I thought I didn't know my ex-husband. Apparently, that simple fact went for my own daughter, too.

Okay, so my state of mind may have been a bit muddled by the time I pulled up to the front doors of Vesterville House. My deep breathing had done a little to calm me down, but I was well aware going into this situation in my present state wasn't the smartest choice I could make.

Didn't stop me from making it.

Lloyd took one look at my expression and moved in fluid rapidity, leading me to the dining room where my two darling girls giggled over a late breakfast, both looking up with surprised expressions when I stopped at the door.

Calliope's happy greeting instantly tanked, her sullen response to my jaw jumping and teeth grinding clench all the answer I needed.

She *knew*.

And hid it from me.

"Your father," I said, needing to stop for a moment to grasp my temper in very firm hands before going on, "already knew about you and Thalia. Apparently, he's known for a year or more." Neither of them spoke, though at least Thalia seemed sad, reaching for Calliope who sat back in her seat with her expression hard and closed, arms crossed, willfulness written all over her. "According to him, he's happy for you both. No, it was the fact you *quit school without telling us*," another pause, another abrupt anger wrangling, "*dumped your scholarship* and *lied to me*," she was a dead child walking, "that was the issue at hand."

She jutted her chin at me, so much her father in that moment I seriously contemplated screaming.

"It's none of your business," she said, "and Dad shouldn't have gone behind my back like that."

"I know," I snapped back. "He shouldn't have. But you know him. He never lets something go if he suspects you're hiding from him. So, the fact you're even angry tells me you've been waiting for this. Right?" She at least looked a little guilty. "That means you purposely lied to me, Callie. I don't care if you ever go back to school. If you live on the freaking street or in this," I waved around me, "fantasy world of yours, but you lied to me." That hurt more than anything I'd ever endured as I sank into a seat, suddenly weak, vulnerable, heartbroken. While my daughter looked away, refused to meet my eyes.

"I've spent my whole life with an FBI profiler needing to know everything," she said, voice surprisingly soft. "And with a therapist overcompensating and giving me free rein to be and do whatever I want, handing me tools and teaching me processes." There was the bitterness. Her head snapped around, gaze flat. "I only ever wanted a Dad," she stressed that hard enough, "and a Mom," she didn't have to be so cruel, did she? "Oh, I know how lucky I am." So much sarcasm. Where had it been hiding all this time? She waved a hand at Thalia who sat in misery, crying silently, looking back and forth between us while Calliope tore my heart from my chest. "Trust me, I've been told my whole life how lucky I am." She stood abruptly, her chair scraping over the wooden floor in a screeching protest. "I'm sick of it. I want to be my own person and it's time you both let me."

She stormed off then, out the glass doors into the garden, Thalia hugging herself while I stared after my daughter. Where had this come from? Who was this girl I didn't know, couldn't recognize? I caught my breath, the sob that wanted to come, as Thalia rose and came to me, hesitant, as though afraid of what I might say, how I might react.

I hugged her tight, Thalia returning the embrace. "She loves you," she whispered. "Things are… she's struggled to tell you the truth. She hated school. Felt obligated, that Trent would be disappointed, that you'd try to fix it." I pulled back, shaking my head, but Thalia's soft, sad smile kept me silent. "I think coming out, admitting to people who we are, that we love one another… it's given her the courage to do that in the rest of her life, too." She squeezed my hands before letting me go. "I'm sorry, Seph. She didn't mean to hurt you. She's been so upset, wanted to talk to you. Didn't know how to and have you just accept without trying to counsel her." Was I that mother? I'd been blaming Trent for his paranoia, for refusing to give her privacy. But had I really been so blind and selfish and indoctrinated by my perfect Mom ideal I'd failed her worse than he had? "Just give her a couple of days to sort through it. You gave her the ability to do that. Trust her to work it out on her own now that it's out in the open."

I think I said goodbye. I don't really remember. I shouldn't have been driving, though, I know that much, still have no idea how I ended up at home, staggering through the door, sinking to the floor and sobbing my heart out.

While Belladonna climbed into my lap and purred.

Looking for more from Persephone Pringle? You're in luck! Book four, ***Better Bones and Gardens***, is available right now!

ABOUT THE AUTHOR

Everything you need to know about me is in this one statement: I've wanted to be a writer since I was a little girl, and now I'm doing it. How cool is that, being able to follow your dream and make it reality? I've tried everything from university to college, graduating the second with a journalism diploma (I sucked at telling real stories), am an enthusiastic member of an all-girl improv troupe (if you've never tried it, I highly recommend making things up as you go along as often as possible) and I get to teach and perform with an amazing group of women I adore. I've even been in a Celtic girl band (some of our stuff is on YouTube!) and was an independent filmmaker. You can check out the whole Lovely Witches Club series for free at:

https://lovelywitchesclub.com.

My life has been one creative thing after another—all leading me here, to writing books for a living.

Now with multiple series in happy publication, I live on beautiful and magical Prince Edward Island (I know you've heard of Anne of Green Gables) with my multitude of pets.

I love-love-love hearing from you! You can reach me (and I promise I'll message back) at https://patti@pattilarsen.com/home. And if you're eager for your next dose of Patti Larsen books (usually about one release a month) come join my mailing list! All the best up and coming, giveaways, contests and, of course, my observations on the world (aren't you just dying to know what I think about everything?) all in one place:

https://bit.ly/PattiLarsenEmail.

Last—but not least!—I hope you enjoyed what you read! Your happiness is my happiness. And I'd love to hear just what you thought. A review where you found this book would mean the world to me—reviews feed writers more than you will ever know. So, loved it (or not so much), your honest review would make my day. Thank you!

Printed in the USA
CPSIA information can be obtained
at www.ICGtesting.com
LVHW020221161024
793958LV00019B/266